TIKI TORCHES AND TREASURE

Gabe Maxfield Mysteries, Book Two

J.C. Long

Dedication

I want to thank the Hawai'i Gang for helping me with this one, as always. This one is dedicated to you guys!

Prologue

WHAT I'VE NOTICED about my time here in Hawaii is that it's certainly never boring. There're lū'aus, surfing contests, tourists to watch; everything you could ever want.

I was in a good place in my life, too. I'd all but forgotten Seattle and the Trevor incident that led to my moving to Honolulu in the first place. I was happy. I had a boyfriend—my gorgeous cop neighbor Maka—and my best friend Grace was cleared of murder charges.

Most of the excitement in my life came from surfing lessons I was getting from Maka and Grace. I honestly think they enjoyed it more than I did. The jobs that came to us at work, when they came, were routine: finding lost puppies and catching cheating spouses in the act, things like that.

The best thing was that nobody had pointed a gun at me or threatened my life in weeks.

I really liked that.

I had no idea as I floundered on a surfboard in the ocean that sunny Tuesday that I was about to find myself in excitement of a very different kind.

A World War II-era tontine.

Buried treasure.

Dead treasure hunters.

Meeting Maka's family.

Boy was I in it deep this time.

Chapter One

I WAS DROWNING.

Salt water burned my nose as I flailed my arms and legs in the ocean, trying desperately to reorient myself. Every time I started to surface, the ocean waves broke over me again and again. I was done for.

When I finally surfaced and the water drained from my ears, I could hear my companions laughing at my expense—my best friend, Grace Park, sounded like she was going to asphyxiate herself from laughing too hard. My boyfriend, Maka Kekoa, at least had the decency to attempt to hide his laughter from me.

"I'm glad my near-death causes you such amusement," I growled, glaring at them as best I could with salt water from the Pacific Ocean stinging my eyes. "I knew surfing lessons from you two was a bad idea."

The three of us were floating in the ocean a ways off from the shore of Waikiki Beach in Honolulu, Hawaii, the city I now called home. Well, I was floating in the ocean, which was where I seemed to spend all my time in these lessons. Maka and Grace effortlessly straddled surfboards, Maka also keeping a tight grip on mine so it didn't get swept away by the waves.

"Don't get frustrated," Maka told me supportively once he'd schooled his face to mask his laughter. "No one does it well on their first try. It's kind of like sex."

I didn't take much comfort from his words.

"How about the four-hundredth time?" I grumbled, swimming to the surfboard. I managed to heave my body onto it, feeling the sun warm my skin. I'd gotten tan torches my month of being out and about in the constant sunshine of Hawaii, and my hair had gotten longer, almost enough to give me the surfer image. Now if I could just stay on the damn board.

"Don't be grouchy, Gabe," Grace chided, splashing water my way. She looked beautiful in the morning sunlight, her dark skin glistening. She wore a teal bikini that showed off her trim, fit form, toned from a lifetime of exercise and the surfing she'd taken up in Hawaii. She was half Hawaiian and half Korean, which is what drew her to Hawaii after we both graduated college in Washington.

"We've been at this for two weeks, and I have improved exactly zero percent." I probably sounded like a whiny kid complaining to them, but I couldn't help it. I hated not being good at something. "I think I'm just not meant to be a surfer."

"Everybody's meant to be a surfer," Maka said, as if I'd made the most ridiculous remark ever. Grace nodded her head in emphatic agreement.

"Easy for you to say," I scoffed, flailing my arms wildly as a wave nearly displaced me from my board again. "You were a professional surfer, remember? And *you*," I rounded on Grace, "were basically born incapable of being bad at something. Me... I'm just me."

It felt strange having a pity party in the ocean on a beautiful mid-October morning. Hawaii was paradise in a lot of ways—the sunshine seemed constant, and at a time when Seattle would already be plunging into a chill that heralded winter, it was warm and pleasant in Hawaii. I wasn't a morning person, though, and Maka and Grace insisted we have these lessons before work. That meant we were usually in the ocean by a quarter to seven.

"You're more than 'just you' to me, babe," Maka assured me with a wink, making me blush.

Maka was full-blooded native Hawaiian, and he had the complexion to prove it, bronzed by a life spent frolicking in the sun and waves. He had broad shoulders and narrow hips and was taller than my five foot eight, with perfect black hair and lush, full lips that were utterly kissable. His deep brown eyes always seemed to twinkle, as if a powerful light danced behind them.

"Ugh." Grace rolled her eyes and pretended to gag.

"You're jealous," I teased, sticking my tongue out at her.

"Jealous of you having to eat the same meal every night, so to speak? I don't think so."

"Hey, if I could eat prime rib every night, I would," I said.

"Did you really just compare me to ribs?" Maka asked flatly.

"Huh? What? No—I was referring to eating the same meal every night..." I trailed off, realizing how it must have sounded to Maka, even though I didn't mean it that way.

"If I'm anything," Maka went on firmly, "I'm loco moco."

I gaped at him for a moment. He had a problem with being called prime rib, but wanted to be a rice bowl topped with a hamburger, a fried egg, and gravy.

"Actually," I said after a moment, "I can see that." And I could. Loco moco was something you wanted to splurge on, something that was decadent, almost sinful. That description fit Maka to the letter.

I tried to give him a smoldering look, but a rogue wave rocked under me, catching me off guard and dumping me once more into the sea.

"Can we *please* call it a day now?" I pleaded once I was back on my board.

Grace looked like she was in no hurry to bring my suffering to an end, but Maka took pity and checked his watch.

"Actually, we should call it a day. I still need to shower and get to work. It's going on nine, now; I can only justify going in so late a few times a week, or the chief gets pissy."

"We also have office hours," I reminded Grace for what felt like the tenth time that week. She was really good at what she did—we were private investigators—but she didn't have the mindset necessary to run a business. That had been handled by her partner before me, and Grace was still getting the hang of being in charge of both sides of the business. Well, partially, since we equally shared ownership and those responsibilities.

"This is what we have a secretary for," Grace pointed out, though she reluctantly began paddling to shore, Maka and I following suit.

"Poor Hayley's only been with us for a week," I panted, tired from the lesson and making it back to shore. "Give her a break."

"Best way for her to learn is to just throw her into the pool," Grace said once we were back ashore.

I didn't respond immediately; I was too busy sucking in sweet, sweet oxygen and hoping my wobbly legs didn't give out as I trudged through the hot, sun-baked sand to the place we'd left our towels.

"I guess it doesn't matter so much," I said when I could. "Business has been pretty slow since we hired her. Not good, considering the office we've got now. Rent's a bitch."

When I'd agreed to be Grace's partner at the private investigation firm she'd been co-partner in, Paradise Investigations, I helped finance a move to a new building, worlds nicer than the one she'd been in before.

We'd had a keen interest in us the first week or so after the move, considering how we were constantly in the news regarding the murder mystery I'd solved to get Grace off a murder charge. The interest had died down in the following weeks; as it stood now, we hadn't taken on a new client in five days, and we'd finished the current projects three days before, which meant three days of no billable hours, and thus no money coming in.

"We could always fire her," Grace suggested, tossing me my towel. "It'd be one less salary we needed to pay."

"That doesn't seem right," I said, though I'd probably consider it after another week of no income being earned. "I'm sure we'll get by."

"We could always take an ad out on TV," Grace suggested suddenly.

"Isn't that tacky?" Maka wrinkled his nose a bit.

Grace shielded her eyes from the sun, squinting at Maka. "It's not like we're lawyers."

"Even if it isn't tacky, we can't afford it," I reminded her as I wrapped my towel around my waist and gathered my board under my arm for the trek back to our cars. "We're going to have to pray someone comes in and offers us a job that isn't finding a lost cat or staking out seedy motels—something we can get some money out of."

Grace grunted, her spirits somewhat dampened by my pragmatism, but I knew she would get over it. This was our relationship, often consisting of her being flighty and dreamy and me being the cord that pulled her—sometimes forcefully—back down to earth.

"Okay, I've got to go," Maka said when we reached his car. "Already running late."

"See," I said, pausing long enough to take a quick kiss on the lips—though I wanted much, much more than a quick kiss—before continuing. "This is yet another good reason we should just stop these morning surfing lessons."

"Not gonna happen. Seeing you dripping wet is worth being late to work."

And again, in the space of ten minutes, I blushed.

"You two are disgusting," Grace muttered.

"Shut up, Grace."

I stood there, grinning and waving stupidly as Maka slid behind the wheel of his car and drove off. Here it was, a little over a month he and I'd been seeing each other, and still I felt that feeling of butterflies in my stomach whenever he looked at me or I laid eyes on him, and I still got that goofy look on my face when he was around. The honeymoon phase definitely hadn't come to an end for me yet.

Grace came to stand next to me, a put-upon look on her face. "Can we go? Or are you going to stand here making googly eyes at an empty parking space?"

"Excuse me?" A quiet voice spoke up behind Grace and me, startling me out of my cloud-nine reverie. Grace and I cautiously turned around to find a bookish man behind us, clutching a newspaper in his hand. His hair was sandy blond and disheveled, his mousy face sunburnt across a forehead made high by a receding hairline and the bridge of his nose, where a pair of glasses that looked like they'd been through the ringer was perched. His clothes were wrinkled and looked like he'd slept in them once or twice.

"Can I help you?" I asked cautiously.

"Yes—well, that is to say I hope so. This *is* you, is it not?" The man held the newspaper out to a small photograph of myself and Grace on the steps of the Honolulu Court House on the day we'd both given testimony in the trial of the man responsible for murdering Grace's business partner, Carrie, and attempting to kill me—three times, I might add. Our testimony was critical in his conviction. That and the fact that he confessed to the crime to Maka and myself in the office of his employer, Mr. Delgado, who was no doubt a corrupt businessman. Actually, Grace and I both thought Delgado was behind Carrie's murder. She'd been investigating *him*, after all.

For a moment, I wondered what our faces were doing in the paper. Had this guy been holding onto the paper for that long? We'd ceased to be relevant pretty much the day after we testified—but then I saw the headline: *Sentencing for Convicted Murderer James Ashford Set to Begin Thursday.* The article no doubt mentioned Grace and me in there, which explained the picture being used again.

Grace threw her towel over her shoulder, tapping her foot impatiently. "Yes, it's us, and no we're not going to make statements about how we hope the sonofabitch fries in the electric chair."

"I don't hope that," I added quickly. "Just so we're clear, when you print that quote make sure it's attributed just to her. Just her."

The man narrowed his eyes in confusion, wrinkling his nose in a way that did nothing to alleviate the mouse-like image I had of him.

"What do you mean? Oh—! No, no. I'm not a reporter. You two run a private investigation firm, correct?"

Grace's attitude and bearing changed immediately at the mention of our company.

"Yes, yes, we do. I'm Grace Park, licensed private investigator, and this is Gabe Maxfield, my apprentice."

I grunted and kicked her foot. I hated when she referred to me that way. She wasn't wrong, technically; I didn't have my license yet, because the process was a long one and required many hours working alongside someone who was licensed. That didn't mean I had to like being called her apprentice. I felt like the word immediately made her the more senior of us in the eyes of clients, and we were equals in the company in everything but licensure.

The man's face lit up. "Wonderful! I have a job I would very much like to discuss with you, one that I think will be quite lucrative for all involved."

The man's enthusiasm made me wary; I couldn't tell if he was just a genuinely enthusiastic guy or if he was pretending to be enthusiastic to cover up how shitty the job he's offering was. The last time a client had been so enthusiastic I'd ended up inside a disgusting-smelling garbage can outside a questionable sex shop in order to catch a man suspected of cheating on his wife with a prostitute who worked there. All I'd gotten from the night was ruined clothes and a crick in my neck. The next day when I'd met with the client, she confessed her information was wrong and her suspicions spanned from a lack of sexual interest that turned out to be because he was suffering from erectile dysfunction and was too embarrassed to say anything.

"Okay, what's the job?" To her credit, Grace didn't sound too over-eager.

The man looked positively startled by the request. "No, not here. Definitely not here. It isn't safe to talk about it here." He dropped his voice low, taking on a conspiratorial tone. "It's too risky; this is very sensitive information."

"Well, then we can go to our office," I offered. "It's not too far from here, and you could follow us..."

The man shook his head, and I trailed off. I was starting to think the enthusiasm wasn't trying to cover up a bad job offer but that this man was totally crazy. I signaled to Grace that we should back away slowly, but the glare she gave me in return didn't leave me much hope that she would do so.

"I'd like to meet with you at this address this afternoon at one, if at all possible." He dug a crumpled-up piece of paper from his pocket and held it out toward me. I took it reluctantly. It was a receipt from a gas station for gas, gum, and a Coke. On the other side, an address had been written in hurried but legible handwriting.

This was too weird—the random address, the paranoia, and the outfit. I felt like I'd suddenly stepped onto the set of a really bad movie based on a Tom Clancy novel. I wasn't much into spy thrillers in my fiction and definitely didn't like the idea of it in my everyday life.

Before I could voice my concern over the matter, though, the strange man turned and hurried off, head ducked low, like he thought someone was keeping an eye on him.

"That was an interesting man," Grace remarked, though her voice carried quite a bit more amusement than I was feeling at that moment.

"Interesting is one way to put it." I stared at his retreating back, an uneasy feeling settling over me.

"Hey, earth to Gabe?" Grace waved her hand in front of my face. "Let's get to work before Hayley decides we're not coming in today and goes home."

WHEN WE ARRIVED at the new office—remodeled from a dentist's office that was remodeled from a residence—Hayley was sitting at the desk that had once been where the dentist's receptionist sat, a book open and her nose buried in it. Other than the grunt of greeting she gave us as we entered, she barely noticed our arrival.

The first order of business was to get out of the damp swimsuit, which was becoming uncomfortable in the air conditioning Hayley insisted on blasting in the front room. Like me, Hayley wasn't a local—someone born in Hawaii who wasn't ethnically Hawaiian—but hailed from Michigan, and she seemed intent on recreating the climate she was accustomed to in our office. I wouldn't be surprised if snow greeted us one day once winter came.

Once changed, I went back out to where Hayley was reading some gay romance fiction of some sort. The front of our office was nicely carpeted—a new one, since the old one was stained by the hordes of kids who'd presumably been forced to the office by their parents—and had nice, moderately priced furniture.

"Any phone calls this morning?" I asked.

"Nope." Hayley didn't even look up from the book.

"So another day with no work."

That did make Hayley look up. "I don't even know what it is you do here."

I couldn't tell if she was joking, and I didn't know which I would find more annoying. "Sometimes I don't either."

"Feels good to get into dry clothes," Grace said, joining Hayley and me. "No calls?" I shook my head. "Bummer."

The nonchalant way she said that bugged me a bit, though I couldn't say why. It might have something to do with how it was mostly my money at risk here.

"You do realize if we don't work we don't make money, right? All that effort we spent moving into this nice building would be wasted."

"You worry too much." Grace perched on the edge of Hayley's desk. "Besides, we have a job."

I raised an eyebrow. "We do? I thought we hadn't had any calls."

"There's always beach guy."

It took every ounce of strength in my body not to literally face-palm. "There is no way in hell we're going to drive off to some address we don't even know to meet up with some weirdo who propositioned us on the beach."

"Why not? You said we need money, and this guy said it would be well-paying."

"He didn't quite say that," I argued. "Besides, did anything about him scream money?"

"You're actually considering turning down a paying job?" Hayley asked, closing her book to give me a skeptical look.

"It's not a job offer," I protested, resenting Grace more than I thought possible at that moment. "It was some random guy approaching us, flashing our picture and telling us to meet him at some completely random location. It wasn't even written on a nice piece of paper, either," I added, brandishing the crumpled receipt he gave me.

"What's the address?" Grace asked.

"422 Ward Avenue," I read off. "You know it?"

Grace thought for a moment, biting her lower lip in concentration. "Ward Avenue rings a bell, but no."

"See?" I said, gesturing vehemently. "This is why we should *not* meet with Mr. Random Beach Man! We don't even know what's at the address he gave us."

"It's the Dustlight Motel," Hayley supplied.

Grace and I were in perfect sync as we turned surprised glances on her. "How do you know that?"

Hayley turned her computer screen in reply, showing a Google Map of the area.

"Well," Grace said, throwing an arm over my shoulder. "A run-down motel is pretty par for the course for us, so I trust you have no more objections, right?"

I groaned. She had me beat, and I knew it. We needed the money, and no matter what weird vibes I got from the man offering the job, it was an offer. We couldn't afford to be picky. "There are days I hate this job."

"Don't be silly," Grace chided, pushing me away from her. "You have to actually do a job to hate it."

"IT'S PRETTY CROWDED for one o'clock on a Tuesday," I remarked as Grace turned her Jeep Wrangler into the parking lot of the Dustlight Motel. It looked precisely how I imagined it would—apart from the rather large number of cars in the parking lot. The building was two stories, shaped like a U written in block letters. Doors ran along the side we could see. Along the section connecting the other two I saw an ice machine, a vending machine, and two staircases. The room dead center was marked Office.

"It's also nicer than some of the places we've caught people cheating at," Grace added, turning off the engine and unbuckling her seatbelt. "Barely, but it is."

I couldn't really argue with her there, with the dirty alley and smelly garbage can still fresh in my mind, so to speak. "Even still, we don't usually go to the dirty motel until *after* we've been given a job. This is a serious breach of protocol."

Grace slapped my shoulder impatiently. "Would you *please* stop worrying so much? We've just come to talk; we haven't agreed to the job, yet. Try to hide how much you hate this until we at least hear what he wants us to do, okay?"

"No promises," I scowled, opening the Jeep's door and stepping out of the car before she could hit me again. I started across the parking lot and then stopped, a very important realization dawning on me.

"Why are you just standing here in the parking lot?" Grace asked, looking at me as if I was crazy.

"Grace, we don't know what room we're supposed to meet in," I pointed out to her.

"Oh. Shit." Grace paused, pushing her designer sunglasses up on her head. "I guess we should just ask for him at the office."

"We don't know his name."

"Shit. Well, we describe him to the guy and hope he's seen him."

I put my hands on my hips. "Do you remember what he looks like?"

"I was kind of hoping you did," Grace said sheepishly.

I sighed, leaning my head back to gaze up at the sky, wishing that God would just let this ridiculous exercise in futility come to an end already. "The only descriptor that comes to mind right now is *weird*."

"Yeah, me too. Do you think there's any chance he'll know who we're talking about if we just say 'a weird guy'?"

"Look at this place, Grace," I said, gesturing at the motel with a wide sweep of my left arm. "Do you think weird is going to be enough?"

"I guess not."

We stood there for a moment, needing to come up with a new plan. My hope was that the new plan involved going home and dialing random numbers in the phone book until we found *someone* who would need our services. I'd rather turn into a telemarketer than go door-to-door in this place hoping for the right guy to open up. I'd heard enough stories from Grace about the sordid sexual lives of cheaters in a place like this, and I didn't want to see anything disgusting that I wasn't being paid to see. I was pretty sure that my insurance plan through the company didn't cover weekly therapy sessions.

Any hope I had of going back to the office was shattered by a voice calling out to us from one of the first-floor rooms near us on the right. "Hey! Hey, over here!" The strange man from the beach had the door barely open, his head poking out of it. He was jerking his head in what I assumed was meant to be a *Come here* gesture but only served to make him seem even crazier.

"See? We're in luck. His room is right there." Grace flashed me her most winning smile before hurrying across the parking lot toward the man.

"You won't say we're lucky when he's murdering us in there."

"You think everyone wants to kill us, Gabe. Then again, with what's gone on with you since coming to Hawaii, I guess it's understandable."

We reached room one nineteen, and the man held the door open for us to slip inside. He closed the door behind me just moments after I stepped inside; it was no doubt my imagination, but I could have sworn I felt the door graze my heel.

The motel room was the same as most motel rooms: one simple queen-sized bed—complete with a scratchy comforter in the ugliest floral pattern that seemed to be reserved for cheap places like this—one closet barely big enough to fit more than two days' worth of clothes, an old beat-up television that still had a VHS player built into it, and the world's tiniest bathroom. In front of the window, a small coffee table that looked like it was more made of cardboard than wood sat, squeezed between two chairs that looked like they would fall apart the moment someone tried to sit in them.

The bed was unmade, the blankets tossed around, pillows wrinkled, and clothes were thrown on the floor carelessly. On the far side of the room, partially shielded from my sight by the bed, I could see bits of an opened suitcase, clothes sticking out wildly. A laptop was perched precariously on the edge of the nightstand, the clock, bulky phone, and a dinged-up lamp pushed aside to make room for it. There were several articles tacked up on a wall, pictures of what looked like World War II maps and a few travel maps of Hawaii.

"This is charming," I remarked, pretty sure my eyebrows had disappeared into my hairline. "And not at all creepy." Grace dug her elbow into my side. "Ow! Stop it."

"Sorry the room is in, er, a bit of a state," the strange man said, wringing his hands together as he looked at us. A long minute passed with him saying nothing. I clasped my hands in front of me, rocking on my feet and waiting for him to speak.

"Okay, Grace, we should really go," I said after the man continued to say nothing.

"No, no, no," the man said quickly, taking a step toward us. I grabbed Grace's arm and pulled her back away from him, and he stopped, wide eyes showing how startled he was by my action. "I apologize for the smoke and mirrors and all the secrecy. I'm sure this must seem quite strange to you."

"Yes," I said while Grace said, "Not at all," in a tone of voice that was completely unbelievable.

"Let me start by introducing myself. My name is Edwin Biers. I already know who the two of you are, of course, otherwise how would I have found you?" He let out a laugh that sounded just shy of manic to me. "Please, have a seat so we can talk business."

I looked around for a safe place to sit. Edwin gestured toward the two chairs on either side of the table, as I'd been afraid he would. I eased myself into it slowly, testing it to see if it would manage to hold my weight. I wasn't all that heavy, being closer to the skinny side of the spectrum than the toned side, but I was worried. The chair wobbled a bit beneath me, but other than that, it held fast. That might have been the first pleasant surprise of the day.

Edwin sat on the bed and crossed one leg over the other, resting his hands in his lap.

"What exactly is it you need from us, Mr. Biers?" Grace asked, not ungently, when the man didn't seem to know where to go from sitting down. "We are a fully licensed and recognized private investigation firm, and we can offer a wide range of services—"

"I'm looking for treasure," Biers said quickly, shocking Grace into silence.

I, however, had no problems finding my voice. The man was insane— there was absolutely no doubt of that in my mind. Driving here had been a huge waste of time and gas. *Thank god it was Grace who drove.*

"I'm sorry, did you say treasure?"

Biers nodded in a way that was altogether too excited for me.

"Yes! I am here in Hawaii right now tracking down a treasure that might be worth millions—maybe even tens of millions of dollars."

I gave Grace the most incredulous look I could manage, and she shrugged in return. She didn't have to say anything for me to know that she was thinking *Just hear him out.* I didn't want to hear him out. I wanted a psychiatrist to hear him out, but not us.

"You're...a treasure hunter?" Grace asked, hesitating as she looked for the right words.

Biers chuckled. "No, not like I'm sure you're thinking. This is the only treasure I'm after—and I've been after it for three years."

"And you need our help?" I asked, not bothering to keep the skepticism out of my voice. "What could we possibly do to aid you when you've been working on this for three years?"

Biers's face fell a little. "It's difficult to do alone. Not that I am alone; there was a group of us. Seven guys, all of us united in the hunt for this treasure. It's proven to be more elusive than we were expecting."

"Makes sense," said Grace, humoring him for a reason that I could not fathom. "Good treasure's got to be hard to find."

"Indeed," said Biers.

"I'm sorry, I'm going to stop you there." I held up a hand to draw their attention back to me. "You said *was*."

"I'm sorry?"

"You said there *was* a group of you. What happened to the group? Did they give up?"

Biers lowered his gaze to the ugly carpet. "No, they didn't give up. Several of them...several of them have disappeared."

"*Disappeared*?" Grace repeated loudly.

"Shh," Biers said, turning his gaze to the door like he expected someone to come bursting in on them then and there.

I was liking this less and less with every passing moment in Edwin Biers's presence.

"What do you mean disappeared?" I asked, voice quieter than Grace's.

"Each of those who have disappeared stopped making contact out of the blue. They no longer respond to any attempts to contact them. I'm worried."

"Worried about what?" Grace asked curiously.

"Maybe they just gave up on your treasure hunt and were too embarrassed to tell you," I couldn't help but add. "I mean, a modern-day treasure hunt does sound a bit on the wacky side. Life isn't an *Uncharted* game." Both Grace and Biers fixed me with blank looks. "What? You don't know the—it's a series of games about—oh forget it. I should have just said *Indiana Jones*."

"They didn't give up," Biers said fiercely, eyes blazing. "Each and every one of us fully believes in this cause."

"So what do you think happened?"

"I think they were murdered."

"Murdered," I repeated flatly. "For the treasure?"

Either Biers didn't notice my disbelief or he didn't care. "Like I said, the treasure is worth a large amount of money. I think someone else is after the same treasure and is trying to take us out before we can get to it."

"So it's a chase to a buried treasure," I said, rolling my eyes.

"Precisely." Biers nodded his head once.

He definitely doesn't understand my sarcasm.

"So, if I'm following you," Grace said slowly, propping her elbow up on the table and her chin on her fist, "now that your friends aren't around—for whatever reason—you want us to help you find this expensive treasure."

"Yes. I'm running out of options." He leaned forward, pressing his palms down on the table and almost unbalancing it; both he and Grace lifted their weight from it quickly. "You're my only hope."

Grace caught my eye, the question clear in her eyes. I shook my head slightly. She frowned, and I shook my head again, this time more firmly.

"We have a retainer," she said, glancing back at Biers.

"I'm afraid I've invested all of my money in this project. However, when we find the treasure—"

"*If* we find the treasure," I corrected sourly.

"—I'll give you twelve percent of the profit."

"We don't work without a retainer. I'm sorry," I said, even though I wasn't the least bit sorry. "Let's go, Grace."

"What? Wait a minute, Gabe!"

"*Let's go, Grace,*" I repeated through clenched teeth. As far as I was concerned we'd wasted enough time on this ridiculous little venture, and I wanted to get back to reality. "Good luck with your treasure hunt, Mr. Biers."

"Huh? Oh, thanks," said Biers despondently. "I'm sure I'll figure something out."

I dragged Grace from the dark motel room and back out into the warm Hawaii sun. *Now I know how Alice must have felt climbing out of the rabbit hole.*

"Thank god we're out of there," I said, making a beeline for the Jeep. I didn't realize Grace wasn't with me until I damn near reached it. "What are you waiting for?" I called to her across the lot.

"Twelve percent of one million dollars is one hundred twenty thousand dollars, Gabe," she said, refusing to move from the shade cast by the second-floor walkway above her. It looked like if I wanted to talk to her, I was going to have to go back. That or shout at her across the lot, which was also a valid option.

"I know how much money it is, Grace, but that only matters if we actually find the treasure. And what are the chances of us finding any sort of buried treasure? Pretty much zero, I'd say."

"You don't know that," Grace argued indignantly.

"He's been looking for it for years, Grace! I don't know about you, but I'd rather *not* spend three years on a wild goose chase—especially since he can't afford to pay us!"

Grace held up her hands placatingly. "I'm not saying we should spend years hunting for treasure. But why don't we at least give it a chance? Put in a week's worth of work, and if we come up with nothing, then that's that. Please?" Grace put her hands together as if she was praying. She even threw in her pouty lips.

"You really just want to be able to say you were on a real treasure hunt, don't you?"

"You got me there."

I sighed, running a hand down my face. "You know what, fine. Fine, fine, fine. A week, Grace," I added as she started jumping up and down in excitement. "One week. Exactly seven days, that's it."

Grace knocked on Biers's door, making little low-volumed sounds of anticipation.

The door opened cautiously; Biers must not have expected us to come back. We had that in common.

"Can I help you?"

"We'll do it!" Grace took Edwin Biers's hand and shook it enthusiastically. "We'll help you find your treasure!"

"For one week," I added, pulling Grace's and Biers's hands apart.

Biers smiled, and it almost made him look normal. "Oh, that's wonderful news! You won't regret this!"

"I'm pretty sure I will," I muttered, but neither of them heard me over Grace's noises and Biers's trying to usher us back into his motel room to make plans. *In fact, I already do.*

Chapter Two

"BURIED TREASURE?" MAKA repeated for the fourth time, looking between Grace and I. "He actually has you two looking for *buried treasure?*"

"Can we stop saying buried treasure?" I pleaded, head in my hands. "Every time you say it I feel worse and worse about this."

Maka, Grace, and I were at dinner later that night. It was a beautiful evening, and we'd taken a table on the patio. Maka was friends with the restaurant owner—he was friends with lots of people, but I'd noticed he had a *lot* of friends in the food business—so the patio was just us, a sign indicating it was reserved for a private party hanging from the door and ensuring our privacy.

It was a beachfront restaurant famous for its fish, and the patio had a wonderful view of the ocean. Clouds had picked up as the day progressed, so I could barely make out the Pacific in the dark, but I could hear the crash and hiss of its ebb and flow quite clearly.

"Stop being such a downer. This is a really cool chance for us." Grace cracked open a lobster claw. "I, for one, am excited about this."

"Oh yeah, what's not to be excited about? We're going to go looking for treasure that probably doesn't exist and make no money while doing it." I violently speared a piece of grilled asparagus with my fork. "Sounds *great.*"

"You know, you could have said no." Grace dug the plump meat of the lobster claw free with the tiny, long fork she'd been provided, dipping it in butter before popping it into her mouth.

"I *did! Three times!*" I cried, banging my hands down on the table and nearly knocking my glass of wine over. It would have tumbled off the table if Maka hadn't caught it. The man had incredible reflexes; if I wasn't so annoyed at my best friend, I would have found that to be quite the turn on.

"It's just a week," Grace consoled. "Chill out. You still know nothing about the Aloha way of life."

"He's learning," Maka said, coming to my defense. "It takes a long time to get into the groove of life here in Hawai'i." He took my hand in his, rubbing his thumb across my palm in a small circle and sending a shiver straight to my crotch. A month with a very active sex life and still the slightest touch from him had me hard in seconds. I felt like I was back at that extremely awkward age where the fabric of my clothes rubbing against my skin gave me boners. Not that I was complaining, though.

"If you say so," Grace muttered before taking a deep drink from her wine glass.

"I just think it's silly," I said, not releasing Maka's hand. "He's thrown three years of his life away looking for buried treasure and now he's trying to get us to waste our time, as well."

"See, this is your problem, Gabe. You seem to be sorely lacking a sense of wonder. Listen to that out there." Grace gestured toward the all but invisible ocean with her wine glass, nearly sloshing some of the red all over the table. "Listen to that magic. How can you sit here beneath the sky in this magical place, smelling and hearing the ocean, and not think about all of the possibilities this world has for us?"

"Just so we're clear, is it the restaurant that's magical or the patio or...?"

"God damn it, Gabe, you know what I mean! Stop being an ass just to be an ass!"

"I think you're a bit drunk," Maka said, no doubt entertained by our exchange. "Did you drive?"

"Why?" Grace scoffed petulantly. "Are you going to arrest me? Wait. With you that's a legitimate possibility. Never mind. Don't worry, I took a Lyft tonight."

"I'm not against the romanticism of the whole thing," I said, trying to get our conversation at least somewhat back on track. I'd invited Grace to join me and Maka for dinner with the intention that Maka help me convince her that taking Edwin Biers's job was stupid. True to form, though, we hadn't really managed to stay on task. "I'm just saying that we need to look at the big picture, that's all. We can't afford to keep Paradise Investigations open if we don't bring in jobs that make money."

"If we find treasure that's worth as much as this guy says, it's going to be no problem! We'll have made up for the time we've gone with no jobs and then some!"

"But Grace, we have to be realistic," I insisted, knowing I was probably fighting a losing battle. Once Grace made up her mind, she was surprisingly difficult to sway. Stubborn, in other words. "What's the likelihood we succeed, that we come across any treasure here on this island?"

"Actually," Maka began, and I groaned, lowering my head until I could hit my forehead on the table. "There's plenty of legends of buried treasure all along the islands, including here on Honolulu."

"How interesting," I said, voice deadpan. "Do tell me more."

Maka reached over and patted my shoulder. "Sorry, babe. I'm just saying that it's not outside the realm of possibility."

"Neither is being hit by a meteor," I scowled, looking up at him. "That doesn't mean I should start preparing for the end of the world."

"Where's your sense of adventure, Gabe?"

"Trumped by my sense of wanting to get paid," I shot back.

"Oh, Gabe," Grace said, voice full of pity. "Such a sad life. Anyway, it doesn't matter," she went on before I could do more than glare at her for her remark. "You agreed to a week, so we've got a week to see if we can find this guy's treasure."

"His own friends don't even want to help him," I reminded her, hoping in vain that I could talk some sense into her. "Why do you think that is, if not because they realized this treasure hunt is crazy?"

"I don't know; maybe because they're dead?" Grace countered.

"Woah, dead?" Maka looked between us suspiciously.

Damn it, Grace. I kicked her under the table. We'd purposefully agreed to overlook the possibility of danger because Maka had been a bit on the overprotective side since my first foray into private investigating nearly got me killed on multiple occasions.

"No one said they're dead," I argued. "They probably just want him to think they're dead so they don't have to go through with the ridiculous treasure hunt."

"So you think Edwin is delusional?" Grace paused, thinking over her words. "Okay, I saw the motel room, so that might not be implausible."

"Can we stop talking about the ridiculous treasure hunt?" I asked, tapping my fork against the side of my plate grumpily.

"Actually, I have something we can talk about," Maka said. Though he sounded perfectly normal, I caught a change in his mannerisms that stood out to me. He was nervous, I would bet anything on that fact.

"What's that?" I asked, lifting my wine glass and taking a drink.

"Well...hear me out. My family is having this big dinner this Friday—they do it at least twice a month."

"Uh huh," I said, keeping my face blank even though I felt a stab of fear. I was pretty certain I knew where he was taking the conversation.

"They've been wanting to meet you since I told them about you, and I figured maybe this Friday would be a good chance for them to do that." Maka didn't quite meet my gaze as he extended the pseudo-invitation.

I felt like someone had punched me in the stomach. Things had been going very well between Maka and I since we'd gotten together. It was my investigation of the murder of Grace's partner that brought me and Maka together. Since then we'd been spending time together, alternating whose condo we stayed in. It helped that we were neighbors. Though we were exclusive, we'd never really talked about reaching more serious levels, and as far as I could tell, meeting the parents was a huge step, and I wasn't certain I was ready.

I didn't know how to say that to Maka, though. I knew from the talks we'd had that his family was very important to him, and he'd be either insulted or crushed that I didn't want to meet his parents. Well, I *did* want to meet his parents, just not at this early stage in the game.

"So," Maka went on, unaware of the storm brewing in my mind and my stomach. "Do you want to have dinner Friday night?"

Shit. Shit. What do I say? I glanced toward Grace. Judging by the look on her face she could see what predicament I found myself in, but there wasn't anything she could say in the small space of time I had, and the longer I went silent the more likely it was Maka would catch on to my uncertainty and misinterpret it.

"Sure," I blurted, forcing a smile on my face. "Sounds like it'll be fun. I'm looking forward to some home-cooked authentic Hawaiian food."

Don't oversell it, idiot.

Maka beamed like I'd just told him the best thing he'd heard all day—and for all I knew, I had. "Great. I'll let my parents know."

"Yeah, great," I repeated, feeling anything but great.

WHEN WE FINISHED dinner, Maka drove me home after making sure that Grace actually got her Lyft ride. He had an early morning the next day, so Maka went back to his place. I didn't really agree with taking on the ridiculous treasure hunt, but once I took on a job, I would put my best effort into it. When we reached the end of the week, I'd make sure no one would be able to say I didn't give it my all.

The first thing I wanted to do was look up as much information as I possibly could on Edwin Biers. I didn't have his social security number or anything we would need to run a background check—we'd get his forms filled out tomorrow and could do the real research then—but I could do a simple Google search to see what came up.

Well, after a shower.

Once I'd washed and dried, I grabbed my laptop and set to work. Edwin Biers turned out to be a fairly common name, and as I started scanning the search results, my mind turned back to Maka's invitation. The moment I even thought about meeting his family, my heart began to race. I didn't have much experience in that department: my only real adult relationship, Trevor, never took me to meet his parents. It made me wonder, at the time, if there was something wrong with me, some flaw that made it impossible for me to meet someone's parents. Was it just so obvious I would be hated?

Would Maka's family hate me? I *was* a haole, an outsider, and for all I knew, Maka's parents wouldn't like the idea of us together. I wouldn't be able to blame them, either, considering outsiders came in and stole this island from the natives and treated them awfully.

Maybe they wouldn't like the idea of him with a private investigator. It didn't seem like such a glamorous job to other people. I mean, it really wasn't a glamorous job, so I couldn't get upset about that. Maybe a private investigator, one who didn't even have his certification, at that, wasn't good enough for their detective son.

Didn't movies and books say that mothers always hated whoever dated their precious sons? That couldn't have just come out of nowhere, right? There had to be a reason for it, I'd imagine.

"God, I don't want to meet his parents yet." I threw myself back on the couch and stared up at my ceiling despondently. I didn't want to meet his parents, but I didn't want to upset Maka, either. Things were going so well between us; I was afraid that saying no would upset that. Grace kept telling me that honeymoon period wouldn't last forever, but that didn't mean I needed to help it along toward its end.

Okay, Gabe, back to work. I sat up, forcing my eyes back to the computer screen, staring at it without really seeing any of the words. I didn't think I'd find anything useful about Biers there; I didn't even have any way of knowing what information was about him. Where was he from? What did he do for a living, other than hunting this ridiculous treasure?

Did I really think that I was unworthy of Maka? The self-doubt about Friday's dinner crept back into my mind insidiously without me even realizing it at first, and by the time I did, I was already skipping down that thought trail at a frantic pace.

Maka was a successful police detective, having risen high in the force at a rapid pace. He'd also been a professional surfer at a very young age. Who was I, other than the son of wealthy people, someone who'd accomplished nothing greater than becoming a paralegal in Seattle?

I solved a murder, I reminded myself. *The cops were going in the wrong direction, and I figured it out.*

But would his parents see me the way Maka's partner—Benet—did, that I was just being a busybody and sticking my nose in places it didn't belong?

More importantly, why couldn't I just let go of this and focus my attention on work? I would be no use to Grace or Biers if every other thought that went through my head was me freaking out about meeting Maka's family.

I wonder how big of a family we're talking here. Four people? Just his mom and dad? Twenty people? Maka hadn't given me any real details, so I had no way of knowing beyond taking a guess. I didn't know much about family gatherings, considering most members of my family couldn't stand each other, but from what I could tell from Maka, it would probably be a large one. Family seemed to be an important element of Hawaiian culture, so I had a hard time imagining family gatherings that didn't consist of the entire family, from parents right down to fourth cousins twice removed.

I was in no way prepared for that.

I forced myself up off my couch and into the kitchen, deciding that if work wouldn't keep me distracted from my more and more panicked thoughts then I would rely on something else to. This morning's breakfast dishes still needed to be washed.

God, it must be bad if I was willing to do the dishes to distract from it; I *hated* washing dishes.

I'd just gotten the water hot enough for my liking and was slipping on the rubber gloves I wore to do the dishes when my cell phone rang. I considered ignoring it, but it was Grace's ringtone. With everything that had happened a month ago, I made it a point to never ignore Grace's call unless I was in bed with Maka.

I tossed the gloves back onto the sink and grabbed my phone from the couch. "Hello?"

"We've got a problem, Gabe."

"Yeah, 'cause that's a great way to start a phone call," I said sarcastically. "What's going on?"

"I just got a call from Edwin Biers," she started, though I cut her off with an exasperated sigh. "Hear me out. He sounded pretty panicked. Said we need to meet him at some cafe right away. I know the place he wants to meet; it's not far from the old Paradise Investigations office. Carrie and I used to get coffee there at least twice a week."

My first instinct was to tell Grace to tell him to take his crazy ass to bed, but it wouldn't be very professional.

"Did he say what he wanted?"

"No, just that we need to meet him right away. These are billable hours, Gabe," she added pointedly, still living under the delusion that we were going to make any money from this ridiculous treasure hunt. I knew it would do me no good to try to talk sense into her; Grace had the uncanny ability to completely dismiss reason and logic when it suited her to do so. "I think we should at least go meet him to see what he has to say. Maybe he's made a discovery in the treasure hunt."

Not likely, I thought. I didn't bother saying it to her, though, since she'd just ignore me. Instead I said, "How are you going to get there? You've been drinking and shouldn't drive. So have I, for that matter."

"Calm down, it's not that big of a deal. It's been more than three hours since we left the restaurant. I'm fine. I'll be at your house in a few minutes. I'm almost there."

Of course she was; why would I think that she'd give me a chance to say no? That wasn't her way. Better to beg forgiveness than to ask permission and all that.

"Fine," I surrendered. "I'll be at the door."

I hung up the phone and started for the door. Before I got there, though, the sound of water cascading caught my attention.

"Fuck!" I'd left the kitchen faucet running.

I rushed to the kitchen and cut the water off, fishing around for the rubber stopper. There was a small pool of water spreading over the counter and floor since I'd gotten there too late. Great. This was turning out to be a swell night.

THE COFFEE SHOP Biers chose was called Coffee Barn and was one of those places that thought it would be frequented if it kept everything in dark wood and operated under a theme. There wasn't a single surface that didn't look like it was taken straight out of a House and Garden magazine feature. Picturesque paintings of pastures and old farmhouses and barns lined every possible surface, and their cups and merchandise all featured a barn and cow logo. Edwin Biers sat at a table meant for two people in the corner of the coffee shop, clutching a mug of tea in his hands. He looked even more paranoid than usual: his foot was tapping constantly, and he kept looking furtively around the coffee shop, as if he suspected that someone in there might mean to him harm.

When I opened the door, he literally jumped, eyes wide like a raccoon who'd been caught in a trash can, uncertain what reaction would be most appropriate now. I could practically see his heart pounding in his chest like he was in one of those old-fashioned Looney Tunes cartoons.

Grace and I made a beeline for Biers, Grace taking the available chair and me standing between them.

"What's going on, Mr. Biers?" Grace asked, removing a pocket-sized notebook and a pen from her purse.

"Someone's following me," Biers whispered. "I don't know when they started, but I noticed them an hour ago. I was on my way to my room when I noticed the car behind me. With the car's headlights, I couldn't see into it, but I got a strange feeling."

Great. We came out here for another conspiracy theory. I wanted to just grab Grace by the arm and drag her out of there after telling Biers to go home, get some rest, and maybe see a psychiatrist while he was at it. The only thing that stopped me from doing so was the way the cup of what I assumed was tea from the lack of coffee smell shook in his hands as he lifted it for a sip. He wasn't just saying this for attention; he was genuinely upset.

That didn't mean that he wasn't simply being paranoid, of course.

"How do you know they were following you?" I asked, trying to keep the disbelief from my voice; based on the reproachful look Grace shot my way, I didn't succeed. If Biers noticed it, though, he didn't show it.

"They followed me from where I was driving, in the heart of downtown, all the way here. I can't see how them being with me for that long can be coincidence." Biers pressed his fist against his mouth, his foot tapping out an even more agitated tempo.

Downtown was a ways from where we were, that much I could admit, but it wasn't entirely out of the realm of possibility that someone from the same area of town Biers had been in wanted to come here.

"They circled the parking lot of this place three times, slowly, before driving away," he added, like that was something important.

I glanced out the window. The parking lot had eight cars in it, and the majority of those had to belong to employees because there were only three occupied tables in the place, counting the one I stood next to.

Grace was following along the same train of thought I was. "Was the place busy when you got here?"

"It was the same." Biers started to lift the tea but put it back down, slipping his hands into his lap beneath the table, probably to hide the trembling.

"What made you come here?" I asked. "We're still a bit far from your room."

"I was being followed! I thought it would make the most sense to go somewhere with people. Then I decided to call you so I didn't have to be alone."

"What is it, exactly, that you're expecting us to do, Mr. Biers?" I asked carefully. I didn't know if he thought we were offering bodyguard services, but he would be out of luck if he did. We were private investigators, and that was it.

"I was hoping you would go with me back to my motel room and make sure I get back there safely." He ducked his head and lowered his voice. Even he must have realized just how utterly ridiculous his request sounded; he was a grown man, asking us to do the adult equivalent of checking for monsters under the bed.

"Fine," Grace agreed, standing up. "Finish your tea and let's go."

"Can I talk to you over here for a moment, Grace?" I slipped my hand beneath her elbow and pulled her off toward the door to the single unisex bathroom in the place. "Grace, we're babysitters, now?"

"We're whatever the client wants us to be," she said, somehow managing to sound snooty when she did so. Did she even hear how ridiculous she sounded?

"I'll remind you of that when he decides he wants someone to tuck him into bed."

"Don't worry, I'll send him your way." Grace patted my shoulder and stepped around me, rejoining Biers. I just stood there for a moment, unable to stop my mind from conjuring a picture to match Grace's words. I imagined how awkward Biers would be in even the simplest act of intimacy; a slight hand touch would probably be beyond his grasp.

Don't take it any further, Gabe Maxfield.

"Gabe, come on, we're ready to go," Grace called, ushering Biers toward the door.

"I'm going to find a way to make you pay for all of this one day, Grace, I promise."

WE REACHED BIERS'S motel room without incident—me driving the Jeep because I still didn't quite trust Grace behind the wheel, considering she'd been drinking.

"See, what did I tell you?" Grace asked, as if the uneventful trip to the Dustlight Motel was something she'd foreseen and hinted at, but I'd only ignored.

"I'm surprised he didn't freak out about us following him and try to speed off," I joked.

"He's our client, Gabe," Grace chastised.

"It's not like I said it to him," I said defensively.

I watched Biers get out of his car and triple click the lock button on his keychain—the horn beeped three times. I was ready to put the Jeep in drive and speed out of there, but Biers stopped in the middle of the parking lot, back to us, staring at his room in the motel.

"Grace, what is he doing?"

Grace frowned, as puzzled as I was.

"That's a good question." She unbuckled her seatbelt and opened the car door. "Come on," she insisted when I didn't move to do so as well.

"Do I have to?" I groaned.

"Just get out of the damn car!"

I sighed and got out, following behind Grace and dragging my feet to make it clear that this was not something I wanted to be doing. I'd go with her, but I'd drag my feet as much as I possibly could.

Grace reached Biers and put a hand on his shoulder. "Is everything alright, Mr. Biers?"

He opened his mouth several times to speak, but no words came out, so he finally just shook his head.

"What's wrong?" I asked, trying hard to hide my annoyance. I didn't want to be standing in the middle of the parking lot of a cheap motel at nine thirty at night talking to this guy. I wanted to be at home where I could at least take my pants off and get comfortable.

"My room," he said, repeating it twice before I finally understood what he meant. "Someone is in my room."

I looked toward his motel room. The curtains were drawn, but light spilled around them. I could see no sign of life or motion or anything else behind them. "How do you know?"

"I never leave the light on," he answered. "It's a waste of electricity. There's someone in my room."

"Then we should call the police," Grace said, reaching for her phone.

"No," both Biers and I said at the same time.

"What? Why?"

"We don't have time to wait for the police," Biers said. "They might find what they're looking for about the treasure while we're waiting for the police to show up."

That wasn't the reason I was going to give, but since Grace would probably go for that one before she went with *The police don't need to be bothered by this ridiculousness*, I nodded my head in agreement.

"We don't even know if someone is in there," I added. "Maybe just this once you forgot to turn off the light."

The look on Biers's face said exactly how he felt about that possibility. I sighed, growing impatient with the whole situation.

"Look, I'm going to go and have a look. Do you have your key?"

Biers looked absolutely terrified for a moment, staring at my hand, extended for him to hand me his room key. He gathered himself after a moment, taking a deep breath, his chest swelling alarmingly, before he shook his head. "I'll go with you."

"You two are crazy not to wait for the police," Grace said, phone still in hand.

"This was your idea," I reminded her flatly. I waited until Biers started toward the door, fishing his key from his pocket, before I added, "Besides, there's no way someone is in there. This guy is nuts, and you know it."

Grace pursed her lips and shrugged. It was crazy, but I was beginning to think Grace was buying into the whole conspiracy theory Biers laid out for us. She'd always been such a rational person before coming to Hawaii, or at least she'd seemed that way to me. Maybe it was because no one had ever come to her with a treasure hunt in Seattle.

Biers slid his card key into the slot on the door and pushed the door open slowly, flinching back like he expected someone to come dashing out of the room toward him. No one did. In fact, I peered over Biers's shoulder and there didn't seem to be anyone in the room at all.

I resisted the urge to say I told you so out loud, though I did shoot Grace a pointed look. She replied by flipping me off.

Biers walked into the room, body tense as he looked around. I couldn't hold back the derisive snort as he opened the closet door and peered inside. I covered it well, though, disguising it as a bad cough. *Please don't look under the bed*, I prayed as Biers approached it. There was no way in hell I'd be able to hold it together if he did that.

He didn't; he sat down on it instead, looking defeated. "I guess there's no one here," he said, sounding almost disappointed that his place hadn't been broken into. Maybe that was his way of being embarrassed about the fuss he'd put up tonight. The clear lack of anyone in his motel room kind of cast his story about being followed into doubt, too.

"You've had a long day," Grace said comfortingly, though how she could know that I couldn't say. "Why don't you get some rest and tomorrow we can get—"

The sound of a toilet flushing silenced Grace. Biers tensed, frightened expression returning to his face. All three of us turned our eyes to the bathroom door, which none of us had bothered to check when we'd arrived.

Biers was right; someone was in his motel room.

Chapter Three

NEITHER GRACE, BIERS, nor myself took a breath as the bathroom door opened and a rugged-looking man in his forties stepped out. He was broad shouldered, had the slightest hint of a paunch beginning, and stocky legs that gave him a boxy shape. His hair was dark brown, though elements of gray could be seen sprinkling throughout it. He also had a full beard, the color slightly darker than the hair on his head. I caught a glimpse of a tattoo on his forearm that looked like it was indicative of some military service, though I couldn't distinguish the branch.

I instinctively stepped between Grace—and Biers, though that was more about his nearness to Grace than any desire on my part to protect him—and this guy. Biers, though, shoved past me and charged toward the guy, exhibiting way more courage than I would have thought possible from him.

My admiration shifted to confusion as Biers threw his arms around him.

"How the hell did you get in here?"

"Gave the front desk enough information to convince them I was meeting you. They gave me the second key."

Grace sidled up next to me and leaned close to whisper in my ear. "Am I missing something?"

"This is my friend Daniel Rice. He's been helping me on this treasure hunt. He's one of the few of us who still stays in contact." Biers patted Daniel's shoulder firmly.

I couldn't help but notice a big change in Biers's bearing now that Daniel was here. He was more open, less paranoid. If I'd met *this* Edwin Biers, I wouldn't have had such a hard time believing his story about the treasure.

"So these are the private investigators you told me about?" Rice asked, glancing us over judgmentally. "The ones who solved that murder a month or so back?"

"That's us," I said. Even to my own ears, I sounded challenging. Who was this guy to look at us like we didn't meet expectations? We weren't the ones going on some crazy, wild treasure hunt. Sure, Daniel Rice *looked* normal, but if he'd thrown his hat in with Biers on this, then there had to be a screw or two loose in there somewhere.

What does that say about Grace and I?

"Is someone going to finally tell us about this treasure?" Grace asked, and I wanted to kick her. The last thing I wanted to do was sit here and talk more about the ridiculous treasure, not at this hour. I wanted to go home and throw myself down on the bed and just pass out.

Biers shushed Grace immediately, racing to the door and pushing it shut, as if he was afraid someone in this out-of-the-way, dingy stop off would hear us. Maybe he thought his imaginary stalkers from earlier were hiding on the floor above, just praying for us to slip up and mention the hidden treasure.

"You'll want to be a little more discreet," Biers scolded. His level of seriousness seemed utterly disproportionate to the subject matter, and I had to bite the inside of my cheek to not tell him so.

"Okay, that's a no," I said, starting for the door. "We'll let you guys do whatever it is you're—"

"We should tell them about it while we have them here," Rice said to Biers, who sighed.

"I guess you're right."

"Great," I muttered.

Biers motioned for us to have a seat, and Grace and I lowered ourselves once more into the same unsteady chairs we'd sat in before, while Biers and Rice sat next to each other on the bed.

"Well, the story begins—"

"Actually," Rice interrupted, straightening up. "How about a drink first?"

"We drove," I politely declined.

Rice shrugged, shuffling to the small, knee-height refrigerator and then taking out a bottle of cheap whiskey. He grabbed the chipped-glass tumblers on top of the fridge and poured a glass for himself and Biers. Once he was seated in front of us once more, Biers started again.

"Daniel and I, along with the other people in our little treasure enthusiast's group, are all history buffs. We met through various forums and engaged in lots of interesting discussions. We'd talk about visits we'd made to famous locations—particularly from World War II—and would show each other pictures..."

"Not to be rude, but can we please get to the point?" I asked, drumming my fingers impatiently on the table. From the affronted looks on Rice and Biers's faces, I realized it probably came off more brusquely than I thought it would and decided to soften the blow a little. "The treasure, I mean. It's late. I'm sure you understand."

"This is how we got started," Biers said, sounding very close to huffy. "We became friends over a mutual love of World War II history. That's also how we came across the story of this treasure."

"We all shop eBay and other online auction sites for things we can get from the time period—journals, newspaper clippings, rare magazines, that sort of thing," Rice explained. "One day I happened to order an assortment of clippings and papers that had once belonged to a World War II soldier who died some time ago, so someone had put up his items as memorabilia on these sites. It looked to be a pretty big box of random things, so I bought it. When it came, I found an old photo and a spiral notebook in the box. Most of the pages had been torn out or stained, but what was left was intriguing. It detailed the makings of a tontine during the war."

"What's a tontine?" Grace asked.

"It's a sort of deal people make where they put money or something valuable in a safe place somewhere, and the last person living in the group gets to collect whatever it is," I explained. Grace raised her eyebrows in surprise. "What? You think I don't know things. I've come across a few references to tontines in law classes. Not to mention on *The Simpsons*."

"The tontine was made between the man who wrote the diary and four other men. It consisted of a variety of things that were stolen from the homes of Japanese occupiers on various islands in the Pacific during the war," Rice went on.

"Are you sure this guy wasn't confusing real life with that episode of *The Simpsons*?" I asked, mind utterly blown that we were actually listening to this story right now. Neither Rice nor Biers responded to my question.

"The unfortunate thing about all of this is that due to the nature of the sell and the damaged condition of the journal, there was no way to identify the writer. He never named his fellows in the tontine and never identified himself, his branch of service, or his regiment. He gave one name, a reference to someone in the group, but it's just an initial and a last name. H. Graham."

"If that's true, then how do you know the treasure is here on Oahu?" Grace asked. The question sent a surge of relief through me.

Thank god she's actually using her brain and not entirely swept away in this ridiculous fantasy.

"In some of the entries not about the tontine, he does reference Fort Shafter," Biers explained.

"That name sounds familiar," Grace admitted.

"If you've ever seen *Pearl Harbor*—the movie, not the base—then you'll know it's where the incoming Japanese attack was dismissed as a fleet of B-17s coming to the island from the mainland, probably California," Rice explained. He'd finished his drink, and placed the glass down on the edge of the small table. The weight of the empty glass was enough to make the table literally tilt, so he quickly took it up again and held it.

"So it's likely the men who entered into this tontine were stationed there." His logic was sound, even if I didn't think the idea of the mission was. The idea had a little more credence with Rice there, though; he didn't give off the same conspiracy theory nut vibe as Biers. It was probably wrong of me to make that sort of judgment call about Biers, having met him only a few times over the course of one day, but I just had to call it like I saw it.

Biers's head bobbed up and down quickly. "Yes! And Fort Shafter is on Oahu, not too far from here."

"And you can't just go and tell the army you want to dig around the base for wherever this tontine might be hidden," Grace mused.

"Definitely not," I said. "Tontines are illegal. The government doesn't like people collecting things without getting their cut of it."

"Besides," Rice added, "even if tontines weren't illegal, the items in this particular tontine *are*. Soldiers aren't allowed to steal, you know. Everything in it belonged to Japanese citizens at the time. I'm sure that the Japanese government would want them back."

"And you're going to make money off the tontine by selling them on the black market?"

"Of course not!" Biers looked absolutely scandalized at the suggestion. "We're going to return it to the Japanese government!"

"Sorry, sorry," I said quickly, holding my hands up in surrender. "I didn't mean to offend you. I just wanted to make sure everyone knew the expected outcome going into this."

"You need not worry about our intentions," Rice said stiffly. "Nor the army, for that matter. The men would have never been able to enter Fort Shafter with any of their stolen loot. They probably buried it somewhere on the island, somewhere far enough from the military base that it wouldn't be connected to them even if it was unintentionally found."

"And you guys happen to have a rough, general idea of where that might be, right?" Grace asked hopefully.

"Not a clue," Biers said. He sounded altogether too cheerful in light of what he was saying, I couldn't help but think.

"You also have no idea how we're going to get paid," I surmised, liking this situation less and less.

"Our plan is to turn the tontine's contents in to the Japanese government," Biers insisted. "The Germans have paid large rewards for the return of art and such items stolen during the war. We hope the Japanese government feels just as willing to pay out."

"On the black market, we could probably make far more money, of course," Rice added, the words carrying the tone of a familiar argument. I didn't know him very well, but he sounded like he was sorry that wasn't the option they were going with. "I'm sure less scrupulous people than us would do just about anything to get their hands on such a gold mine."

"Speaking of," Biers said, face growing somber. "I was followed today, by at least two men in a black American-made car. I couldn't see their features, but I'm positive they were following me."

"Maybe this treasure hunt has gotten you stressed out," I offered, hoping there was some chance of me getting them off the phantom conspiracy theory. "It might have just *looked* like they were following behind you."

Biers couldn't have given me a more condescending look if he tried, I thought. "I wasn't imagining it! I suppose you think I'm just imagining the disappearances of my friends, too?"

Now that you mention it. I opened my mouth to say just that, but Grace kicked the side of my leg under the table. I gritted my teeth, growling at the pain, and fixed a scowl on her.

"It's gotten worse than you know," Rice said before I could tell Biers just how crazy I thought he was. "Tolly's dead."

Biers gasped, hand—shaking once more—flying up to his mouth. "Not Tolly. What happened?"

"He called me a few days ago, said he'd tracked down a few items he thought might be part of the tontine. He's one of our fellow crusaders, for lack of a better word. He's been working on lists of things reported stolen from Japanese residences during the war," Rice explained to me and Grace. I could see a question forming on Grace's lips, so it was my turn to kick her.

"Ouch! Sonofabitch!" Grace swore, nearly jumping out of her chair. Maybe I kicked her a little harder than necessary, and maybe I enjoyed it, but I wasn't sorry.

"Ignore her," I said, gesturing toward Grace. "Go on."

"I went to meet him, see if he'd come up with anything interesting. He lives in Los Angeles, so it was on my way here, anyway. When I got there, I learned from his husband that he'd died in a car wreck the same day he'd called me. His husband said he'd been frightened, said someone was watching him."

"If he died in a car wreck," I said carefully, not wanting to sound insensitive to their loss, "what makes you think it was foul play?"

"It's not just coincidence it happened on the same day he tells me he made important finds," Rice snapped.

"What *were* his important finds?" Biers asked eagerly.

Rice's face fell at that. "I don't know. His husband couldn't find the paperwork he'd printed off, and his computer was missing, as well."

I blinked, unable to come up with an argument to that. When you threw in missing friends, missing paperwork and computer, it did start to look pretty damn strange.

"Poor Tolly." Biers sighed before taking a deep drink of his whiskey. When his shudder subsided, he added, "And Tolly's poor husband, too. They've only been married two years."

"If you think this Tolly guy's been murdered you have to tell the police," I said firmly.

"Gabe is right," Grace said, her voice a fair bit gentler than mine. "We could talk to Gabe's boyfriend, Maka—he's a cop."

"Tolly's death was in Los Angeles. The police here can't do anything about it anyway." Biers rose and began pacing the sparse space between the foot of the bed and the television stand. "Besides, they'll never believe us unless we tell them about the tontine."

Probably not even then. Some things didn't need to be given voice, however, so I said nothing.

"We can't do that!" Rice cried, leaping to his feet. He marched right up to Biers and grabbed his shoulders firmly, even gave him a little shake. "We've worked too hard on this, Ed. If we tell the police now, we can kiss that tontine goodbye. It will become some full-fledged investigation and goodbye reward."

"But Tolly and the others," Biers whined, shoulders slumping. "Is it worth it?"

"We owe it to them, Ed. After what they've sacrificed, it would be an insult to not find this treasure."

"These guys are intense," Grace whispered to me. "I feel like I'm watching bad daytime television."

"You're not watching it; you're in it," I reminded her. "And it's all your fault, too, remember."

I stood up then, motioning for Grace to do the same. "Listen, Mr. Biers, Mr. Rice, thank you so much for telling us about the treasure and your friend. We really do appreciate it, but it's late, so I think Grace and I should be heading out. I'm sure you've got a lot of catching up to do, anyway."

"Yes, certainly. Okay." Biers grasped my hand in both of his, shaking it overly vigorously. I cringed inwardly because his palms were both moist and clammy. He released my hand and moved on to Grace. Before I could blink, though, Rice had my hand for a shake as well. At least his hand was dry. "We'll contact you tomorrow about getting to work on this."

There weren't words that could adequately express just how glad I was when we stepped out of that room and the door shut behind us.

"I can't believe I let you drag me into this," I complained. "Those two are wackos, chasing after a tontine that might not even exist, or may have already been collected by whoever the last-surviving member of the tontine was."

I tossed Grace her keys, no longer concerned with her blood alcohol level since we were pushing midnight. I was too tired from being in the same room as those two and their manic energy and just wanted to relax on the ride, if possible.

"I think it's kind of exciting," Grace said after several moments of pleasant driving, the only sounds that of the radio—volume turned down low—and the tires on the road.

"I think it's ridiculous," I muttered, staring at the taillights of the car ahead of us. The brake lights blazed to life, bright and red, as the car came to a stop at the light.

"Some part of you must be taken in by the romantic adventurousness of it all," Grace insisted. "Buried treasure, stolen during a time of war, hidden for the last living member of a blood pact. It's like something out of a Robert Louis Stevenson book."

"Yeah, all we're missing are pirates." I rolled my eyes.

I think my sarcasm was lost on Grace; she perked up at the thought, pointing at me. "What about the guys following Edwin today? And the ones that Tolly guy mentioned to his husband before he died? Maybe they're the pirates."

I pinched the bridge of my nose. "You've been marathoning *Black Sails* again, haven't you? There are no pirates after Edwin Biers. And for another thing, pirates usually work at sea, remember?"

"You don't believe him about the men, do you?"

My first instinct was to say "Of course not," but I thought about it for a moment. I didn't give much credence to his story about being followed, just like I didn't trust his story about someone breaking into his room. Then again, I'd been wrong about that one. But the intruder turned out to be one of his compatriots, didn't he? Maybe it was Rice following Biers before.

But why didn't he say so when Biers brought it up, then?

When combined with what Rice said about the Tolly guy, though, I couldn't dismiss everything Biers said entirely.

"I'm not convinced," I said at length. "But if it's true and someone *is* following and/or killing them, then that's all the more reason to not get involved with this case. It's bad enough they've got us hunting for an illegal tontine; I don't want to put my life as well as my freedom at risk."

IT WAS ALMOST one in the morning before I finally crawled into bed and nearly two-thirty before my racing thoughts let me get any sleep. I couldn't chase away the concern that Grace and I were getting into something that was deeper than we would like.

If I die, I thought at one point, *it's going to be entirely Grace's fault.*

When I did finally fall asleep, it was restless, filled with ominous dreams I couldn't remember and didn't think I wanted to.

I woke up to the sound of my bedroom door creaking open. My heart leapt into my chest and I sat straight up, trying hard to see in the dark. My night vision was terrible, though, so I didn't see more than a big shadowy blur.

"I'm sorry," Maka said softly, his comforting voice helping to soothe my thundering heart. "I didn't mean to scare you."

"It's okay," I murmured before falling back onto the bed and staring up at the ceiling. A quick glance at my clock told me it wasn't even six in the morning yet.

The bed shifted beneath Maka's weight as he sat down on the edge of the bed. "I was thinking we could get out to the beach, maybe have a surfing lesson without Grace. See if you respond to a different style of teaching." There was enough suggestion in his voice that I could imagine his eyebrows waggling comically.

"As tempting as that sounds, I'd much rather stay here in bed." I reached out and grabbed his arm, trying to lever him down into the bed with me. He allowed me to do so, shifting further onto the bed so I could rest my head against his chest, using his bicep as a pillow.

"Long night?" Maka asked.

"Yes," I said sleepily, already close to drifting back to sleep.

"What happened?" Maka's voice sounded like it was coming at me through a very long tunnel, and it took me a minute to process the meaning of those two simple words.

"Tomorrow talk about it," I mumbled, unable to keep my eyes open. "Now sleep."

"There are things we can do that are better than sleep," Maka suggested, planting a kiss against the side of my head.

"Nothing better than sleep," I said, and crazy as it might sound, I truly meant it. As beautiful as Maka was, as sexy as I found him, at that moment literally nothing could have made me forego what sleep I could get then.

"Understood. You mind making some room?" When I didn't reply and didn't budge, Maka used his considerably greater strength to move me until there was enough room for him on the bed. He lay down beside me, turning me gently so I was on my side, his body curled behind me.

The man was a heat rock, and though that might bother me at times, it just made me feel safe and comfortable right then. I fell back asleep to the sound of Maka's steady breathing and the feel of his heart beating against my back.

Chapter Four

I WOKE TO an empty bed, Maka having already left for work. I'd been out of it enough that I didn't even stir at his departure, which was unusual for me. I categorized myself as a light sleeper in most situations. I guess that's how much everything about yesterday drained me.

I lay there in bed, staring off at nothing until my alarm went off five minutes later. It took more energy than usual to force myself out of bed. Everything with Biers, Rice, and their ridiculous tontine made me dread the day of work ahead.

I dragged my feet in the shower and then again getting dressed—anything it took to delay the inevitable mental torture to come as a result of spending the day with Biers. His constant paranoia grated on me, as did his obsession with this tontine. It seemed incredibly risky, even if the treasure proved to exist. I couldn't imagine what came after finding it, but I didn't think it was going to be as simple or smooth as Biers and Rice seemed to think it would be.

Once dressed, I stood in the kitchen, staring at the stove. *I wonder if I have time to make some French toast? Then again, I don't know how to make French toast. But you know what they say, no time like the present!* I would do pretty much anything to avoid going to work as long as we had this Biers job.

As pleasant as the idea was, I knew Grace would kill me if I left her alone with Biers, and I probably didn't have any of the ingredients I'd need to make French toast, other than bread and syrup, and that just didn't sound as appetizing. Instead I grabbed a pack of Hostess Mini Banana Nut Muffins on my way out the door.

I was turning into the parking lot of Paradise Investigations when my phone rang. It was Grace.

"I'm just pulling in," I said as soon as I hit Talk so that she didn't have a chance to berate me for not being there. "I'll be in in a sec."

"Pulling in where?" Grace asked. "I don't see your car."

"What do you mean where? At the office, of course." I glanced around the parking lot—the *empty* parking lot. "Now that you mention it, I don't see your car."

I could practically hear Grace cringing through the phone. "Did I forget to text you? I knew I was forgetting something. Sorry."

"Just tell me what you forgot to text me." I rested my head on the steering wheel. The day hadn't even really gotten started and it was already going downhill fast.

"Biers called me this morning. He wants to work at the coffee shop we met him at last night."

Kill me now. "What's wrong with our office?"

"I don't know. Something about being afraid Hayley's been compromised; I wasn't listening very closely."

"Let me get this straight: he thinks our secretary is conspiring against him?" *Please,* I prayed—begged, even—*someone kill me.*

"Does it matter? If he wants to sit at the Coffee Farm and—"

"Coffee Barn," I corrected. "What kind of a name for a coffee shop is Coffee Farm?"

"Like Coffee Barn is much better. The point is, if he's paying for it, we're doing it. Get over here as fast as you can. Did you bring your laptop?"

"Yes, I brought it," I said through gritted teeth. "I'll be there in fifteen minutes."

My mood soured as I drove to the Coffee Barn. I honked the horn at four different cars, and I rarely used the horn as a driver. Maybe the Honolulu traffic was finally getting to me, or I was just being pissy. Either was a possibility at that point.

It wouldn't be the first time I worked on a case away from the office for a client—most of our work required it. That didn't usually involve research, in my experience thus far, and it certainly didn't involve Edwin Biers.

I arrived at the Coffee Barn fifteen minutes later. Grace and Biers had claimed one of the large tables meant to seat five or six people, spreading old newspapers, notebooks, and paperwork across it. Daniel Rice was nowhere to be seen. That disappointed me a little bit, because I liked the calming influence Rice had over Biers.

Maybe he's in the bathroom, I thought wryly. Given my luck, though, I doubted he'd turn up.

"There he is," Biers said brightly, as if I were a friend finally showing up to the bar for drinks and not an employee showing up for a serious research mission. Well, as serious as researching a probably non-existent tontine could be. "Go on to the counter and order some coffee; it's on me, since you're on the clock."

"I'm fine," I said stiffly, even though I could have used a drink of some kind. I looked at the table, searching for a place to put my laptop. Grace saw my look and hurriedly cleared some space, shuffling paperwork and old newspapers aside. I noticed she'd cleared a space on the other side of herself, ostensibly putting two chairs between me and Biers, who sat on the other side of the table. Hopefully this meant we would have very little interaction.

"Are you sure? Okay, well, whenever you want something, just go get it. You ready to get started?"

"Sure," I said, hoping it sounded sincerer than I felt. "What do you want us to do?"

"Well, right now we're going to focus on our only lead: H. Graham." Biers patted a beat-up marble notebook in front of him. Its pages were worn and faded, its cover tattered, most of it missing. The pages revealed beneath the cover were almost translucent with age, the ink long ago dried. "It's the only hope we have of actually figuring out who the people involved are, since no one else is named. If we can find out who they were in connection with Fort Shafter, we might be able to find evidence that will lead us to the location of the ton—er, the prize."

"We've got a name to hunt down," Grace said, cracking her knuckles and then opening her laptop.

"No, we've got an initial and a last name," I corrected. I was really annoyed by the way she kept passing the job we'd taken as something easy or normal when it was anything but. "I don't have any idea how common the family name Graham might be, but for all we know there's thirty thousand H. Grahams who served in the military during World War II."

"I find that unlikely," Biers said, surprisingly apologetic to be disagreeing with me.

"My point is this isn't going to be a quick undertaking. You've had this journal for three years, right? How would you classify the level of success you've had in this?"

"Gabe, come on. Lay off." Grace touched my arm as she spoke.

"No, no. Mr. Maxfield has done nothing wrong," Biers said quickly. "He's right to express his concerns, and of course he's right that I cannot claim we've had any success with this venture until now. But if I'm being honest, we didn't really focus any attention on the name until quite recently."

The fact sounded utterly ridiculous to me. "You had this massive clue hanging over your head for this long and you didn't bother looking at it? Mind if I ask why?"

"We were aware just how difficult the task would be to track down this guy's name. The majority of our work has been spent tracking down possible items that might be in the tontine, as well as trying to narrow down the area the treasure might be." Biers stopped for a moment, realizing how much he'd said, perhaps, and glanced around quickly to see if anyone was nearby.

The Coffee Barn was mostly empty—a back table had two men sitting at it, both of them busy perusing the sports pages. A lone woman sat at another table, earbuds stuck in as she ate what looked like extra thick pancakes. The people there couldn't be less interested in us, and there wasn't a person sitting within two tables, so I didn't understand his need for concern.

"It seems like you were working backwards," Grace observed, tapping her ballpoint pen against the palm of her hand. "It doesn't do you very much good to know what's in the damn thing if you don't know where it is."

Biers smiled, the slightest hint of bitterness there. "We realized that eventually. We were able to narrow the possible location of the item to Honolulu; it just made the most sense based on the information we gathered. After that we started studying maps of what the island was like back during World War II compared to today's modern developments."

"A map's a map," Grace said quizzically, still drumming her pen on her hand. "Why would it matter?"

"It would be unfortunate if they managed to find the treasure and realize it's buried under what's now a Walmart," I explained dryly. "So today we're looking for information about this H. Graham guy, in the hopes that if we somehow manage to find out who he was, we can then track down who was in his unit who he might have gone into this deal with. And from there—from there, what? How do you know there aren't still four men out there waiting for their friends to die so they can collect the tontine? It's not outside the realm of possibility. Or—"

"Or perhaps someone has already collected it?" Biers finished my question for me, his eyebrow raised. "Do you think this is the first time in three years we've had these questions raised, Mr. Maxfield?"

"I have absolutely no idea what you have or haven't discussed with your fellow online history-buff friends, Mr. Biers," I replied stonily, meeting his gaze without blinking. If he'd entered into this agreement thinking Grace and I would somehow just cow-tow to everything he told us, the whole *the customer is always right* nonsense, he was sorely mistaken, and I wanted to make sure he knew that, just in case Grace had given an impression otherwise the previous day.

Biers leaned forward, resting his forearms on the coffee table, his expression at that moment the most serious I'd ever seen. "If you're concerned about being paid for this, you'll be paid either way, Mr. Maxfield. Whether we find the thing or not. If we do, your percentage of it will be added *on top* of your normal hourly fee."

"That makes me feel the slightest bit less nervous," I said sarcastically, though it was half true. It would be easier to focus on this ridiculous farce of a job if I knew I'd be getting paid for it anyway.

"If that settles everything—" Biers straightened up again and reached for a stack of old papers. "—let's get to work."

THREE HOURS LATER, I had a much better appreciation for just how difficult it is to do any sort of research on the internet regarding soldiers in World War II when the most you had was a letter and a last name. There was no rank, no indication of *when* he was actually active and stationed at Fort Shafter. For all we knew, he was only there for a few months before being transferred to the European theater. The longer we spent buried in websites and registries and lists, the more depressed we became.

The only bright moment I had in the entire three hours was when I got a text message from Maka.

Date night tonight. Sound good?

I grinned, heart fluttering when I saw the message. *Sure*, I typed back. *When?*

The reply came less than a minute later.

Knock on my door at seven-thirty.

There was a light at the end of the tunnel, finally something I could look forward to. The impending date night with Maka would make the time spent doing this somewhat more bearable.

"I thought it would be easier to find," Grace complained toward the end of the third hour, slumping back in her chair and rolling her neck.

"What gave you that idea?" I asked with a snort. "More than sixteen million Americans served in World War II, Grace, and Graham is a pretty common surname for people from England and Scotland. We've got our work cut out for us."

"Keep your voices down," Biers said suddenly, barely moving his mouth as he spoke. "I think the men at the table over there are listening to us."

It was all I could do not to roll my eyes in disgust. I couldn't believe we were back on the paranoia already. A quick glance at the table showed me all I needed to know: the men were still sipping at their coffee, engrossed in the papers in front of them. There wasn't the slightest indication they had any interest in what we were talking about or doing. We probably looked like normal college kids working on a project or something. All right, being in my late twenties probably meant I no longer looked anything like a college kid, but a guy could dream, right?

"I don't think they are listening to us, Mr. Biers," I said as patiently as I could.

"They haven't turned a page in the paper in at least thirty minutes," Biers argued. "I've been keeping an eye on that ad right there on the part of the paper hanging off the table. Whatever they're doing, they're not reading."

"Well, if they are listening to us, they aren't getting much information," I said shortly. "This approach isn't working, Mr. Biers. There's just too much to look through and not enough to look *for*. I think we should step away from this and try for some other approach."

Biers started to say something and then stopped, body deflating like a balloon with its air let out. "Maybe you're right; it was stupid of me to think we'd find anything in such a short amount of time. I was hopeful, though."

"Any idea what the next step is?" Grace asked, sounding relieved that we would be setting aside the research for the moment.

"Actually, yes. When we realized what we were looking for was bound to be situated here on Oahu, we reached out and started talking to someone who knows the island well, its history and its area."

"So there's more than the seven you told us about?"

"Yes. Alvin Liu is newer—only about nine months of involvement compared to the three years the rest of us spent, so we don't really count him amongst the original number."

"Okay, he's not one of the original Beatles, I get it," I said impatiently. "But he's real, he's doing stuff, and he lives in Honolulu?"

Biers nodded. "He does. I was set to go see him sometime today, anyway. Maybe we can go on and make that trip now. Perhaps Alvin can give us something new to go on." Biers began hurriedly stacking and straightening the papers he had spread over the table. "Once we're in the car, I'll give him a call and let him know we're coming by."

"Let him know *we're* coming by?" Grace repeated with the barest hint of a frown. "I assumed we'd be going back to the office..."

"I would much prefer it if you came with me," Biers confessed. "I don't much like going to meet new people face-to-face; terribly bad nerves, I'm afraid."

I slid my laptop back into its case, trying desperately to think of some way or another to get out of going to meet yet another wacko like Biers.

Inspiration struck, and I asked eagerly, "What about Mr. Rice? Couldn't he go with you? You three *are* part of the same group, after all, and Grace and I are outsiders." I hoped that would sell it, since it was barely past noon and there was a chance Grace and I could go back to the office and be there in case a not-crazy job turned up.

"I don't know where Daniel is," Biers confessed. "I haven't seen him since not long after you two left the motel. He followed behind, saying he had more work to do. I would feel much better if you two came with me—and besides, this way I won't have to repeat everything I hear from Alvin to you. I'll even drive so you can conserve gas."

I really didn't want to, but he didn't give us much of a choice, so I nodded.

"Let me just lock my computer up in my car and I'll be ready to go."

Grace and I stashed our things in our respective vehicles and found Edwin Biers standing next to a plain rental car, the sort of car that would blend in on the road because of just how little it stood out. It was a muted-gray Japanese-made sedan that looked like the sort of car a financially conservative family of four would drive around during a Hawaiian vacation.

I really hope this guy can afford us.

Biers was already in the car, waiting for us to get in. Grace and I had a moment of silent battle, both of us wanting to sit in the backseat. Of course we decided to handle the situation like adults; at practically the same time, we both took off running for the car.

I didn't realize until it was too late that Grace had the advantage, being on the outside; there was one of those cement blocks holding a streetlight directly in my way. I would have to go around it and lose precious time, and she'd reach the car before I did.

That's exactly what happened, too. Grace stuck her tongue out at me as she pulled open the back driver's side door and slid into the car.

I slowed down, no longer in such a hurry. *How bad would it be if Grace and I* both *sat in the back?* I didn't think that would be the polite thing to do, though, so I reluctantly climbed into the passenger seat. Biers now had a pair of glasses perched on his nose that simply did not suit him, and he was tapping his thumbs nervously on the steering wheel.

"The men from that table walked out just after we did," he said, fear making his voice nasal. "I didn't see which car they got into."

"Don't worry about those men," I told him. I think I did a pretty good job of keeping my impatience in check. "I'm sure they were just heading back to work or something. Lunch break's probably over; you know how it goes." I couldn't tell through the sunglasses, but I was pretty sure that Biers was glaring at me. However he felt, though, he put the car into gear and backed out of the parking space.

"Is it far to this Alvin Liu's place?" Grace asked, words seeming to echo in the tense silence that fell between Biers and me.

"I don't know; I've never been there. I programmed it into my phone's navigation, though." Biers fiddled a bit with his phone until his navigation app came on, highlighting a route. He placed it on one of those detachable phone mounts made for your car that stick on the dash. "The directions say twenty minutes. He lives out in Pearl City, it looks like."

"Good, I like Pearl City." Grace stretched her legs out, looking like someone going on a fun outing instead of work.

"Where is Pearl City?" I asked. My image of Oahu was still that of a tourist: Honolulu and beaches. I knew there was much more to the island, but I hadn't ventured past the main city, except for one time with Maka to go to an authentic lū'au, and I couldn't point out where that was on a map. I was terrible with general orientation and directions, so I heavily relied on my TomTom navigator.

"It's to the northeast of here. It's a residential area—good shopping, too. Nothing very tourist-centric there, either, so you don't see many of the stop-and-gawkers." Grace leaned forward to look at the cell phone directions Biers was using. "This isn't great. It has you taking 91 for part of the way, and you save some time if you just hop right on I-H-1."

"Where?" Biers asked, and Grace expertly directed Biers to the proper interstate. Once we were en route via I-H-1 Grace caught my eye in the rearview mirror and gave me a little nod, which I returned, mouthing *Thank you.*

The first few minutes were quiet, and I dared to hope that things would stay that way, but my hopes were soon dashed by Biers's startled cry.

"What? What is it?" I asked urgently, heart racing, trying to find the source of Biers's reaction.

"Look!" Biers jammed a finger toward the rearview mirror.

I looked in it, trying to see what he was talking about. "All I see is Grace's big head—"

"Jerk," Grace muttered in response.

"—and a normal car."

"What color is the car?" Biers demanded, starting to sound hysteric.

"It's black," I said, and suddenly I saw where he was going with this. "A lot of cars are black, Mr. Biers. It's the most common color for cars in the world, I think."

"Look at the driver," Biers instructed, eyes flicking between the road and the rearview mirror a little too much for my liking.

"I think you're overreacting," I said, trying to keep him calm and failing miserably.

"Look at the damn driver!" Biers shouted, the outburst surprising me. I reluctantly turned and peered back toward the car following us. It was hard to see with the sun beaming down on the window, but when I did catch a glance thanks to an eighteen-wheeler speeding past us, I felt my stomach drop just a little.

"Okay, I don't want you to freak out," I said, using the sort of voice I'd heard people use with animals they thought might go wild. "It's the people from the coffee shop."

No sooner had the words left my mouth than Biers sped up, sending me back against the seat. I watched the odometer reach unsafe levels as Biers swerved between two cars in order to put some distance between us and the car.

"I think this qualifies as freaking out," Grace chirped from the back. She had one hand braced on the seat in front of her, the other on the door. She kept craning her neck to see if the car was following. "I think it's okay; they're not actually—wait, there they are."

I groaned. Sure enough the black car appeared in the rearview mirror, speeding to catch up with us.

"Maybe they're just driving fast, too," I suggested, even though I no longer believed that either.

"Let's find out." Biers jerked the wheel to the right, getting in the furthest outside lane. The black car did the same thing. Glancing at me from the corner of his eye, the short look clearly saying *I told you so*, Biers sped up, and the car behind us followed suit.

There could be no doubt now: we were being followed.

"I can't believe it," Grace crowed, excited. She actually clapped her hands. "We're in a high-speed chase!"

"How can you be enjoying this?" I asked, wincing as Biers maneuvered through a gap between the cars to shake our tail.

"How are you not? This is just like a movie!"

"My boyfriend is a cop! I don't think I'm allowed to get into high-speed chases."

"Would you two *please* keep it down? I'm trying to drive here!"

No matter how fast Biers drove, or how well—and I hated to admit it, but he was a damn good driver—we couldn't seem to get rid of the pursuing car.

"I feel like I owe you an apology," I told Biers, holding on to the dashboard for dear life.

"You definitely do, but now is not the time. I'll be sure to give you a thorough I told you so if we reach our destination."

I blinked for a moment, mind stuck on one particular word in his last sentence. "Did you say *if?*"

"Take this next exit," Grace cried suddenly, sticking her torso between the front seats, seatbelt unbuckled despite the circumstances. She pointed her finger toward the sign for an upcoming exit. "But wait until the last possible moment to do so. Maybe they'll miss it."

"It's worth a shot," Biers said, tightening his grip on the wheel. His voice had a forced calm to it, but his knuckles were white on the wheel, clenched so tightly I was surprised we hadn't heard them snap yet.

The exit rapidly approached, and with each yard, the distance closed and my heart crept further into my throat. A thousand car crashes from dozens of different movies and television shows played over and over in my head, each one more violent than the previous.

I'm going to die. I'm going to die in a fiery explosion, and it's all Grace's fault.

I closed my eyes as the moment came, unable to watch death looming toward me. I heard the squeal of tires as Biers jerked the wheel suddenly, the momentum throwing me around and causing my seatbelt to tighten up. I felt the car waver on the brink of leaving Biers's control, and all sound was drowned out, save for the beating of my heart and the pulse of blood roaring in my ears.

"Oh my god," Grace said at last, voice quivering, though if it was from fear or excitement, or a mixture of both, I couldn't tell. "We made it."

I opened my eyes when I felt the car slow down. I was greeted not with a blazing fireball and the sight of crunched metal and shattered glass but a busy pedestrian street.

We were alive, by some miracle.

"Did it work?" Biers managed to stutter out after several false starts. "Did we—did we lose them?"

I couldn't move; my body still would not respond to my brain, so I left it to Grace to check. She slid down into the backseat and peered through the back window.

"All clear," she announced after a moment. All three of us sighed in relief.

"Grace, I have a favor to ask you," I said when my throat loosened and I could speak again.

"What's that, Gabe?"

"Don't mention this to Maka."

ONCE WE'D ALL calmed down, Grace navigated us toward Pearl City. On the way Biers called Alvin Liu up to let him know we'd be coming by, but there was no answer.

"Perhaps he's eating lunch or something," Grace offered.

"Well, he'll open the door when we get there," I said, mood subdued. I still felt the adrenaline from the car chase, but it was waning and tiredness settled in its place.

"Unless he's not home," Grace said, having quickly regained her normal composure. The woman had to be made of ice.

"He better be home after all we just went through," I grumbled. "Which we're going to need to have a talk about at some point," I added. "We could have been killed."

"That will be the same conversation where you apologize for thinking I'm crazy, yes?" Biers asked coolly.

I fidgeted in the seat. "I said I apologize."

"No, if I recall correctly, you said you *owe* me an apology. Not the same thing."

I was spared the indignity of apologizing right then by Biers's phone loudly announcing we'd reached our destination. We'd driven three houses too far, based on the addresses on the homes, so Biers turned around and brought the car to a stop in front of a nice suburban home.

Alvin Liu lived in a ranch house, painted white with green shutters, a garage on the side. Space was at a premium, considering Oahu was an island, so the yard was small—but it was still a hell of a lot bigger than the small stretch of grass between my condo building and the parking lot.

"His car is in the garage," Biers said, nodding toward the red Prius tucked inside. "At least we know he's home."

On the way up the perfectly cobbled pathway to the house, Grace and I fell back so Biers could take the lead.

"We really need to reconsider this job," I told Grace, making sure my voice was low enough that Biers couldn't hear.

"We agreed to a week," Grace reminded me, as if that was the end of the discussion.

"That was before we knew about the crazy people and their desire to kill us," I argued. On the porch, Biers glanced back at us curiously, and I gave him a small nod of encouragement. Shrugging a bit, he rang the doorbell.

"He told us about this the first day we met him."

"Yeah, but I didn't believe him!" It was remarkably difficult to shout at someone in a whisper, but I think I managed it. "I thought he was crazy, and so did you."

"That's what you get for not giving someone the benefit of the doubt," Grace said haughtily, while on the porch Biers rang the bell again.

"You thought he was crazy, too," I repeated petulantly.

Grace ignored me, walking up on the porch next to Biers. "He isn't answering?"

"No, I don't know why; he should be here, since his car is here." Biers sounded worried. I had to bite back the thought that he was overreacting. I'd thought the same thing at Coffee Barn and look what happened. It was a bitter pill to swallow, but I had to admit Biers wasn't as crazy as I thought. He still seemed pretty crazy to me, though.

"Maybe that's his wife's car," I suggested.

"Alvin never married, as far as I know," Biers said. He stood up on his tiptoes to peer through the window at the top of the wooden door. "It looks like no one's home, so maybe he's walking, or...wait. I see something. Looks like something is knocked over. *Oh god.*"

Biers dropped back from the door before throwing it open and hurrying into the house uninvited.

"We can't just go into this guy's house," I called, peering around to see if anyone was watching.

"Like you haven't done this before," Grace scoffed. She hesitated only a moment and followed Biers inside.

I hate these guys so much. I couldn't let Grace just go running in there without me. Steeling myself, I walked into the house.

The interior was nice, if simple. Unlike most homes, I saw no photos along the walls to show off family or loved ones. The furniture inside was dated, everything feeling impersonal. The room directly to the left was a living room, the right was a dining room that had been transformed into an office. A knocked over potted plant lay half out of the doorway, half into the foyer. That must have been what Biers saw.

I walked into the office and almost ran into Grace. She was frozen in place. I sidestepped her, a bad feeling settling in the pit of my stomach. "Oh fuck."

On the floor, a pool of blood spread on the carpet around a man's body, like a macabre version of the halos that were always painted in renaissance paintings. Alvin Liu was dead.

WE WAITED FOR the police to show up after I called them, being the only one who appeared to be in any condition to do so. The whole situation felt like a repeat of the Carrie incident, just in a different place.

"Don't go in there again," I instructed Grace. Biers had already crossed the threshold, but I could keep Grace out of as much trouble as possible—again nothing new.

"It's different from Carrie," Grace said, voice sounding hollow. She kept staring at the body, a distraught Biers sitting next to it. "I've never seen someone who was shot in real life before."

Alvin Liu hadn't just been shot, he'd been shot in the side of the head. Amongst the ever-growing halo of blood was no doubt bits of bone and brain matter. He still clutched the gun in his hand.

"Let's step outside," I said gently, grabbing Grace by the shoulders and literally leading her outside. I didn't realize until we stepped into the fresh air how heavily the copper scent of blood hung in the house. Now that I did, though, my stomach gave a rebellious lurch.

"There was a hole in his head," Grace said, which did not help my stomach's delicate state. "Just...a hole."

Don't throw up, don't throw up.

"Why would this Alvin Liu guy commit suicide?" I wondered aloud, more to get my mind off the blood halo and gray matter—*Stop, Gabe. Don't lose it.*

"Alvin didn't kill himself," Biers said from the front door, startling me. His voice carried a noticeable tremble.

"He wouldn't do that. He was far too dedicated to this, and to his life in general."

"Suicides can be unexpected even for people who knew someone very well," I said carefully. "You admitted you didn't actually know Alvin, wouldn't call yourselves friends like the others."

Biers was off the porch faster than I expected, getting right up in my face. "You think it's just coincidence another person who was working with Daniel and me on this tontine turned up dead days after I spoke to him—especially considering what David told us about Tolly!"

"Did you notice the gun in his hand?" I cried. I'd been through too much for a Wednesday, and it was all this guy's fault. "He's got the gun in his hand, for fuck's sake! Would you pull your head out of your ass long enough to realize someone is *dead*?"

"The police are here," Grace said pointedly, physically pulling me back from Biers. "Let's just get this over with, okay?"

I was relieved the police who showed up didn't include Maka, but that relief was short-lived. I spent the next hour and a half answering questions that came at us very quickly. Biers handled himself surprisingly well, not even hesitating when he explained he'd been intending to visit Alvin, an old friend, and that he'd hired Grace and I and we were accompanying him on an errand relating to that.

We all gave statements about our whereabouts for the last twenty-four hours, and then it was done. The car ride back to the coffee shop where my car was parked was agony. Anger boiled just below the surface, anger at Grace for getting me into this, and at Biers for every other part of the last two days.

I practically took off running for my car and didn't look back. It was just after four, which meant I had time to go home and sink into a bath, wash away the lingering memory of blood and tension before my date with Maka.

I stayed in the bath until I was prune and withered up and the water had begun to cool. After that my intention was to find absolutely any reason at all that we should quit the job Biers brought us and do literally anything else. There had to be *someone* willing to pay us to do something that wasn't this. As distasteful as I found staking out sex hotels for signs of cheating husbands-to-be, I'd gladly take a dozen of those jobs right now if it meant I could kick Edwin Biers to the curb.

I dialed the office, certain Hayley would still be there. Sure enough, she answered the phone after only two rings.

"Hello?"

"Hayley, remember what you're supposed to say when you answer the phone? You're supposed to say 'Paradise Investigations, how may I help you?' Remember?"

"It's just you calling," Hayley said.

"But you couldn't have known that when you picked up the phone," I said impatiently.

"I saw your number on caller ID."

I frowned. "We don't *have* caller ID."

"Then I have ESP."

"Hayley!"

"Okay, okay, sorry. I'll start saying the stupid thing. You guys should really get caller ID, by the way."

"I'll take that under advisement. What I wanted to—"

"Paradise Investigations, how may I help you?" Hayley interrupted in a chirpy voice that was somehow unsettling.

"*When you answer the phone, Hayley.*"

"I'm just trying to do a good job, Gabe," Hayley said, her voice giving away just how much she was enjoying screwing with me.

"Thank you, Hayley. You're doing a wonderful job. I was calling to ask if anyone has—"

"Nope. No calls and no walk-ins. Is it always this quiet? Are you guys going to be able to afford to pay me?"

"That's a good question," I muttered. "Thanks, Hayley."

"You guys should seriously consider the caller ID. It like, comes with most phones nowadays," Hayley said right before I hung up on her.

It seemed like no matter how much I wanted to we still couldn't afford to get rid of Biers. Life really sucked, sometimes.

Chapter Five

I TRIED NOT to, but I ended up falling asleep on the couch and not waking up until ten after seven. I spent a moment panicking—I was supposed to meet Maka at his place in twenty minutes, and I wasn't ready—and then kicked into preparation mode. It didn't take me long to settle on what I wanted to wear: a navy-blue polo shirt and a pair of white pants.

I brushed my teeth, made sure my hair looked good, and had three minutes to spare before it was time to go next door to Maka's. There were a lot of upsides to your boyfriend literally living next door to you—aside from the obvious sexual ones, of course. I never really had to worry about being late to meet up. Those three minutes gave me enough time to reconsider my pants. I decided to change them, got halfway to the bedroom, and then decided *not* to change them. As I walked out the door to go to Maka's, I kind of regretted not changing them, but there was nothing I could do about it then.

Maka threw open the door right before I knocked, startling me a bit.

"Were you watching through the peephole for me?"

"What? No, of course not. I just have *excellent* sense of timing." Maka winked. "Are you ready to go?"

"I am."

I studied Maka as we made our way to his car in the parking lot. He was dressed in a cream-colored long-sleeve V-neck shirt and nice-fitting denim jeans. No matter what Maka wore, it always looked like he'd stepped out of a catalogue for designer clothes. There was no way I could compete with that, so I just did my best to look halfway presentable next to him.

I was no longer regretting the pants.

Maka drove us to what turned out to be a sushi restaurant in the heart of downtown Honolulu. The streets were jam-packed with cars, the sidewalks overflowing with people—a lot of them no doubt tourists. I caught hints of music playing from restaurants. On the same street as the sushi place, there was also a popular family restaurant chain, a Korean restaurant, and an artisan pizza place. Here in all the lights of glowing signs, it didn't even really feel like night.

"I hope you like sushi," Maka said as he killed the engine.

"Love it," I confirmed, my stomach already growling in anticipation.

The restaurant's interior was set up like an authentic Japanese sushi place I'd been to once: a single long bar-like counter with fourteen chairs in front of it. Behind the counter, two sushi chefs stood waiting to prepare orders as they were made. The wall behind the chairs featured a beautiful replica of a woodblock-style painting of Mount Fuji. All but three of the chairs were occupied by diners, mostly couples engaging in an enjoyable evening out.

A Japanese man stood near the door as we entered. He was probably in his late-fifties, I would guess, with salt-and-pepper hair that looked fetchingly distinguished on him.

"Good evening, gentlemen. Do you have a reservation?"

Maka nodded. "It should be under Kekoa."

The man's eyes lit up. "Ah, Detective Kekoa. Come this way." He led us to two seats in the exact middle of the counter and motioned for us to sit. "These are the best seats in the house," he confided, voice pitched low so others wouldn't hear.

Maka chuckled. "Thank you very much."

The man returned to his post by the door, and I turned my attention to the menu. It was expensive enough that there was no ala carte pricing for the sushi listed, just the single meal options of ten pieces or twenty pieces.

"So are you feeling hungry or really hungry?" Maka asked, noticing the same thing I did.

"Well, considering how much you eat, I think I'll get the twenty pieces and whatever I don't eat, you can eat for me," I said wryly. "I can't imagine twenty pieces being enough to fill you up."

Maka placed our order to the sushi chef in front of us who immediately began to prepare the first dish. While he was busy, I set up the dipping saucers for the soy sauce.

"About Friday," Maka said, and I almost spilled the soy sauce everywhere. It was amazing the effect two little words could have on me: a knot grew in my stomach and I would have sworn I'd broken out into a sweat. "My family usually gets together at about six-thirty. We won't eat until around seven, but my family likes to talk—especially my mother."

"Wait, I have to talk to them?" I said faintly, a pathetic attempt at a joke, and followed it up with an even more pathetic laugh. I was *not* doing a good job of acting nonchalant about this.

The sushi chef delivered our first plate of sushi, *toro*—the fatty belly of a bluefin tuna.

"Are you nervous about meeting my family?" Maka asked after wolfing down his sushi. I still had a mouthful of toro, but before I could swallow it down to answer, the wasabi hidden on the fish struck my tongue, making my eyes water.

"No," I gasped, diving for my water glass.

"Are you sure? You're acting like someone who is nervous."

"I'm not nervous," I insisted. The next piece that came our way was hamachi, or yellowtail. I savored the piece, and not just because I needed a pause in the conversation, either. Hamachi was my favorite type of sushi.

"I am kind of nervous," I admitted when the sushi was gone. I watched the chef making our next dish, uni—sea urchin. I didn't want to see Maka's anger or disappointment, if it was on his face.

"I've never done the whole meet the family thing," I confessed. "None of my relationships were anywhere close to that level."

"Not even Trevor?" Maka's voice dripped disdain whenever he mentioned my previous boyfriend, who'd mooched off me for a long time before draining my bank account and leaving me. Trevor was the reason I was in Hawaii in the first place but Maka didn't seem inclined to thank him for that.

"You know what our relationship was like," I muttered, nodding my thanks to the chef when he delivered the uni. "Trevor didn't let me in to any part of his life he couldn't benefit from in some way. He never met mine, either. Then again, that didn't really have anything to do with our relationship as much as it does mine with my parents."

"Listen, you don't have any reason to be nervous, Gabe. I don't know what you're expecting from this, but it's not going to be some sort of trial where you're given seven thousand questions to determine how well we match. My family isn't like that. They just want to see you, since I've talked about you so much."

His words made me feel bad about overthinking this whole thing with his family. I was probably overreacting to the situation, panicking because of what it might mean about our relationship. To be honest, the only idea I had of this came from television, and in those instances, it pretty much always went horribly wrong.

"You're right. I shouldn't be nervous. It's just...this—us—means a lot to me. I really don't want to do something to mess it up."

"*U'i*," Maka said with a lopsided smile.

"What does that mean?" I asked suspiciously.

"It means beautiful," Maka said bluntly. "You're too cute. I don't think you could do anything to make my family not like you, Gabe."

I ducked my head, a habit I'd picked up with Maka that allowed me to hide the blush his compliments always brought out in me. Wasn't so necessary with my new tan, but habits were hard to break.

"I'm being dumb," I started, but Maka shook his head firmly.

"You're not being dumb. You're being like practically everyone else in the world. Relationships scare just about everyone. Well, except me," he added with a faux-superior look. "Nothing scares me."

I quirked an eyebrow at him. "Oh yeah? What about seagulls?"

"I'm not scared of seagulls. That's ridiculous," Maka scoffed loudly as the next fish—sea bream snapper, called *tai* in Japanese—was put before us. "I just don't like them. They're dirty and carry diseases. Perfectly reasonable."

"I don't know; you seemed pretty afraid to me when that seagull started flying around us at the beach last week," I teased.

"They carry diseases," he repeated in exasperation.

"I know, I know." I decided to take it easy on him, considering how nice he was being about the whole meeting his family thing.

The next dish was delivered and I made a little noise of appreciation. "You know you're in a real swanky sushi place when they give you this," I said, gesturing toward the sushi before us. It was kani nigiri, crab leg. "This looks like real crab leg to me, not imitation stuff."

"Damn right. No fake crab for us."

Cucumber rolls came next, presumably to cleanse the palate. Maka started to say something, and I could tell it was something that had been on his mind for a while. "I came across an interesting report filed out in Pearl City today."

And I thought no conversation with him could scare me more than the family dinner. I'd been wrong, as I so often seemed to be.

"Pearl City?" I repeated, giving him Bambi eyes. "Where's that?"

"You're not that good an actor, Gabe."

"I think you'll find I'm an excellent actor," I huffed, biting into one of my cucumber rolls with a loud crunch. "Okay, fine. I know what you're going to say—and it was entirely a coincidence."

"You've coincidentally ended up at two crime scenes since you've been in Hawai'i," Maka pointed out. He snagged my last cucumber roll and tossed it into his mouth before I could protest.

"So I've got terrible luck," I admitted.

"I'll say. From what I can tell you're not a suspect this time, since it's been ruled a suicide."

"Did they find a letter?" I asked, hoping I didn't sound too hopeful. If they had, it would be indisputable evidence that Alvin Liu killed himself. Even Edwin Biers wouldn't be able to argue with it. It would also once and for all silence his conspiracy theory, or so I hoped.

"Not that I've heard," Maka said, voice turning suspicious. "Why?"

"I was just asking," I said quickly, not wanting to get into it.

"Gabe." I knew that voice. There was no way he would let it go without me talking about it. It was part of Maka's detective nature; he didn't let go of a suspicion until he learned what he wanted to learn.

Over the next three sushi dishes—salmon roe, eel, and squid—I explained Biers's conspiracy theory once more, adding in what we'd learned from Daniel Rice about that Tolly guy. I hesitated and decided not to explain the tontine.

"So you want a note to shut this Biers guy up," Maka surmised when I was finished.

"That about covers it."

"Listen, Gabe," Maka's face took on that no-nonsense look it carried when he was talking as a detective and not as my boyfriend. "You need to *not* get involved in another police investigation. It's bad enough you were at the scene—"

"Trust me, I agree with you," I muttered. "I want to get as far away from this thing as possible. The last thing in the world I want is more guns pointed at me."

"Promise me," Maka insisted.

"I promise I'll stay out of a police investigation." It was a promise I had every intention of keeping. But, like I said, my luck wasn't that great, and I had no reason to believe it would change now.

THE NEXT DAY was a well-deserved day off for Maka, which made it very difficult for me to drag myself out of bed and away from his warm—and naked—body. The sooner I went in, though, the sooner I could tell Grace we were officially done with this tontine nonsense.

"Where do you think you're going?" Maka asked sleepily when I tried to lever myself out of bed.

"I've got work," I said, putting up a token resistance as his strong hands dragged me back down onto the bed. "If I'm late, who knows what Grace is going to sign me up for next."

Maka just grunted, his hands tracing along my arm and across my chest, leaving goose bumps in their wake. His lips started behind my ear and trailed down the side of my jaw to my neck, where his teeth got involved, nipping at the tender flesh there. His touch lit a fire in my blood and sparked a very noticeable reaction in my cock.

"I have to go to work," I repeated, though I made no move to resist him.

"You can't go like this," he said, one hand drifting down to my now prominently throbbing cock. "What would Grace say?"

"I don't really want to think about Grace right now," I said, rolling my head back against his shoulder as he slowly worked his hand over my erection, now slick with pre-come. "But I think you're right. I can't go to work like this."

"I'll help," Maka offered, voice husky with lust.

"I don't have a lot of time," I reminded him even as I thrust myself up into his hands.

"It doesn't have to take a lot of time." Maka captured my lips and shifted from behind me, letting me fall back against the pillows.

I looked on as Maka reared over me, his beautiful body exposed for my viewing pleasure: the dark, sun-baked skin, the large swell of his pecs, topped with pointed nipples, the jutting hardness of his cock.

This must be what it feels like to be hypnotized, I thought as his eyes met mine and held them. He maintained eye contact as he leaned down, until his mouth was just over the head of my cock. I could feel his breath ghosting against it; my cock twitched and I grunted in sexual frustration.

Maka understood and moved his mouth down around my cock, taking it all slowly and carefully. I bucked my hips involuntarily, making him sputter and pull back before glaring at me.

"Sorry," I said, blushing. "I didn't mean to."

Maka went back to work laying a strong arm across my hips, effectively immobilizing them. He took his time for a few minutes, putting his heart into it. The feel of his warm, wet mouth, the expert way he used his tongue to tease the underside of my cock at just the right time, the perfect amount of suction—it was all heaven.

Maka might have remembered that time was a factor, or he might have just decided to pick up the pace. Either way he was soon working my cock rapidly, left hand fondling my balls while the fingers of his right hand teased at my hole. The moment his thick index finger penetrated me, I was undone; my inner muscles clamped down hard on the tip of his finger, my balls drawing up. I barely panted out enough warning for him to remove his mouth before I began unloading.

In the aftermath, I lay there, my body limp and sticky. Maka slid up next to me and planted a kiss on my lips. It was soft and undemanding, despite how much he must have also been aching for relief.

"You've made a bit of a mess," he observed. "Maybe you should take a shower."

"Maybe *we* should take a shower," I corrected pointedly.

A smile slowly spread over Maka's lips. "Aren't you late already?"

"True," I said shrugging. "What's the worst Grace can do? Get a move on, mister. You can scrub my back."

I WAS IN a much better mood when I finally arrived at work just before ten. Even the sight of Edwin Biers on the couch in the front room couldn't bring me down too much.

"There you are!" Grace leapt off Hayley's desk and stomped toward me. I couldn't help notice Hayley wasn't in. "Where have you been?"

"I got held up," I said, knowing Grace would immediately know just what held me up. I had to act quickly to keep her from sinking her jaws into it. "Good morning, Mr. Biers. Grace, where's Hayley?"

"I sent her home for the day," Grace said, glancing toward Biers. "I guess there are some things we need to talk about here."

"At least that means we don't have to pay her," I muttered.

"Okay, I'm just going to start talking," Biers said impatiently, jumping up from the couch. "I already told Grace this, so I'll just tell you quickly. I know that visiting Alvin Liu didn't pan out, but I think we can recover something from that."

Goddamn it. "Listen, Mr. Biers, I don't think this is a great idea, after everything that's happened."

"Alvin Liu was doing research for us," Biers continued as if I hadn't said anything. "I know for a fact he stored everything on an online Cloud server, so even though he's dead, we can still find what he was researching."

"Do you know the password to his Cloud? Or even what Cloud server he used?" I asked flatly.

"Well, no," Biers admitted.

"So we're actually no further than we were yesterday." I rounded on Grace. "Look, I know we agreed to a week, but after yesterday, I don't want to do anything else. These guys have us looking for a needle in a haystack, Grace. All we've got to go on is a moldy journal entry, an old Army photo, and a name that has been pretty much impossible to track down! Sure, we've got a Cloud server now, but we've got absolutely no way to access it!"

"That's not exactly true," Grace said sheepishly. "I've got a guy who does exactly this sort of thing for me—for us, now. He's our go-to tech guy. His name is Jin Hamada."

Something about the way she said the name made me suspicious. I knew Grace very well, and she was pretty bad at hiding certain things, especially in the realm of men.

"So Jin Hamada is your tech expert," I repeated, crossing my arms over my chest. "Just your tech expert?"

"Yes," Grace said, eyes darting away from mine.

"Grace,"

"Drop it, Gabe," Grace said, turning to Hayley's desk. "Besides, I already called Jin. He's on his way here." She shot me a sly look. "Maybe you shouldn't have gotten held up this morning."

"Worth it," I shot back without missing a beat. "When was the last time you got held up at all?"

She scowled. "Low blow."

Biers looked between the two of us, trying to follow the thread of our conversation for a moment before giving up. "Listen, Mr. Maxfield, I know how you feel about this."

"Good. That means I don't have to worry about hurting your feelings," I snarked.

"First you're going to listen to me," Biers countered, voice as commanding as I'd ever heard it. It was enough to give me pause and allow him to barrel on. "I know you don't believe in this—you think you're the first person to call me crazy, make fun of this dream? Frankly, I don't give a fuck. You're being paid, and you're going to damn well do what you were paid for."

Anger lanced through me, white-hot like lightning. My jaw tightened. "Is that so?"

"We have a contract. You've agreed to work for me for one week. It hasn't been seven days yet, Mr. Maxfield. To break it now would be a breach of contract."

I blinked a few times, trying to process his words, the veiled threat within them.

"You want to talk about breach of contract?" I advanced on him. "You withheld vital information—which means you led us into a contract on false pretenses. *That's* a breach right there. If you decided to make an issue out of it, you'd not come out successful."

"I might not be successful in a legal setting," Biers admitting evenly, "but your business would suffer. How difficult would it be to get clients if your reputation's been damaged by even the idea that you've breached your contract?"

"You sonofabitch." I reached for Biers, but Grace grabbed my arm and restrained me.

"We've talked it out, Gabe," Grace said in her *please stay calm* voice. "We're going to check out the lead that we get from the Cloud drive—"

"If we get a lead," I corrected tersely.

"—and if nothing comes of it, he's agreed to say we've fulfilled the terms of the contract."

"How generous of him," I said sarcastically.

"I'm not a bad guy," Biers said quietly, regaining that distracted, paranoid air he'd had when we first met. "I'm just desperate."

And pathetic, I wanted to say, but fighting with him would get us nowhere and might land me in jail. I didn't think Maka could—or would—date an inmate.

"If by the end of the day, we don't have any leads on the tontine, that's it—we're finished. I don't care if you sue us or not."

"That's fair," Biers said after a moment. He tried to sound confident, but it was easy to pick up the thread of fear that underlined his words. He probably clearly saw the end of his fevered and ultimately fruitless search rapidly approaching, knowing there was nothing he could do to stop it.

Looking at a man who was facing the death of his dream, I felt the first stirrings of pity, perhaps even sympathy. I tried to imagine what he must be feeling and couldn't. I couldn't think of anything I'd ever poured so much of myself into.

Maybe I should try to be a little nicer, I thought. *Just a little.*

"So," I said, opting to sit in Hayley's chair, "when is this Jin Yamada guy coming?"

"*Hamada*," Grace corrected, probably without thinking. I gave her a knowing look, and she just clicked her tongue dismissively. "I called him about forty-five minutes ago, so he should be here soon."

As we settled in to wait, Biers went back to the couch. Not wanting to be just sitting out there until this guy arrived, I went back to my new office—anything to keep busy and keep distance between Biers and myself. Sure, I'd decided it might be good to be nice to him, but that would be a lot easier if I kept contact with him to a minimum.

Thinking about Biers made me think about Grace and how this was entirely her fault. I'd only been joking when I told Maka I didn't know what Grace would agree to without me there, but now I could see it could really be a serious thing. She and I would need to have a discussion soon if this working arrangement between us was going to function properly.

A knock came at my door, and Grace poked her head in. "Gabe?"

Think of the devil and she shall appear.

"Yeah?"

"Jin just got here."

I couldn't hold back a sigh. "Okay."

Grace fidgeting uncomfortably for a moment. "Gabe, listen, I'm sorry. I feel like I'm partially to blame for this."

Partially? "You are," I said, but my tone was light and free of rancor. I even smiled a little when I said so. Grace had always been very good at knowing when it was best to apologize to get the least possible verbal thrashing. Add that with the fact I had a hard time staying angry with her and you had a bad recipe—or a good one, if you were Grace. "Come on, your guy is here. We can talk about this later."

"He's not my guy!"

"Sure," I teased, nudging her with my elbow as I walked past. "Let's not keep Mr. Hamada waiting."

JIN HAMADA WAS average height, maybe a few inches shorter than me, with a slender build. His hair was shoulder length, the lower quarter dyed a very striking blue. He had his hair pushed back behind his right ear, revealing three piercings. His short-sleeve Metallica shirt showed off a partial tattoo sleeve on his left arm. He exuded this confident but laid-back vibe, and when he smiled, it was hard to imagine anyone not liking him.

I could see what attracted Grace to him, definitely.

"Aloha, Grace. Long time no see," Jin said when he entered, holding out his fist for a bump. I could have sworn Grace went pink when their fists made contact.

"I know, sorry. Thanks for coming."

"Anytime." He turned to me, appraising carefully. "This must be the new business partner. I'm Jin Hamada. Nice to meet you."

"Gabe Maxfield," I said as we shook hands. "Nice to meet you too." His grip was strong and firm. For the first time ever, I found myself approving of a guy Grace was interested in. The world was getting stranger and stranger every day.

Grace introduced Biers next. "I'll let him fill you in on the details of the job, since he knows them better than I do."

Jin wasn't looking at me, so I made a mocking face at Grace so she knew I knew the real reason she wanted Biers to tell it: so she could just sit there and look at Jin as he leaned his hip against the receptionist desk.

Grace made an ugly face in return, lifting her fist in a subtle warning, before smiling once more when Jin glanced at her.

I paid little attention as Biers explained everything to Jin, instead watching the tech expert and Grace. There was heat in Jin's gaze whenever he looked at her. It struck me that there was something between them that hadn't been explored.

Maybe they need a little help.

"Can you access his Cloud drive?" Biers asked when he finished.

"This isn't exactly a legal thing that you're asking me for," Jin observed.

"And we'll pay the usual fee," Grace said. I wondered what his usual fee would be that it would make him okay with doing something of questionable legality.

"We'll double it," Biers added, desperate for Jin to say yes.

Jin let out a low whistle, which made me think that Grace paid him a lot of money.

"Damn, that's tempting. But no, the usual fee will be fine. Do you know his IP address?" He received a blank look from Biers. "Okay, then...do you know his email address?"

"Yes, that I do know." Biers found a pen and piece of paper to write it down for Jin. "How quickly can you get the information?"

"Let's not get ahead of ourselves here. There's a lot of Cloud servers out there. I've got to figure out which one he used. It's going to take a little time."

"We appreciate it," Grace said before Biers could start whining. "Really, we do."

Jin gave her a boyish smile and shrugged. I wondered if either of them knew just how into each other they were. "It's cool. Beats doing website building and maintenance. I'll keep you updated."

"Yes, do, please," Grace said so eagerly I cringed. "Keep me updated as much as you can—or need, I mean," she added. I wondered if she felt more embarrassed than I did for her.

Assignment received, Jin set off to earn his money.

I'd hoped for a bit of down time to tease Grace about Jin, but it wasn't to be. The door had barely swung closed behind Jin, figuratively speaking, before Daniel Rice showed himself again. He was wearing different clothes than we'd seen before and had dark circles under his eyes, hair a bit of a mess.

"Daniel, there you are!" Biers jumped up and hurried to his friend. "Did you hear about—"

"Alvin? Yes. I saw it in the paper. Suicide? I can't believe it."

"You shouldn't, either. It wasn't suicide."

"That's not what the police say," I interjected. There was only so much insanity I could handle. "The police say it was a suicide; no sign of a struggle, no sign of forced entry, and there was gunpowder residue on his hands, Mr. Biers."

Biers opened his mouth to argue, but Rice put his hand on his shoulder, shaking his head.

"Listen, I came by because I think I finally did it—I finally have a lead on H. Graham."

The mood in the room changed instantly. Biers looked excited, Grace intrigued. Me, I just felt this sense of foreboding.

"What?" Biers sputtered. "Where? How?"

"One question at a time," Rice said calmly. "I've been looking through residential records and birth certificates and such. I found an H. Graham living here on the island who served at Fort Shafter during World War II. He moved here after the war—maybe he liked the island a lot and decided he wanted to live here. The way I found him was through a search of newspaper databases. It was his obituary that I came across."

"He's dead?" Biers looked crestfallen—no doubt at the prospect of his lead being gone and not the fact that a man was dead, I'd wager.

Rice nodded solemnly. "His family still lives in Kapolei, though."

"Where's Kapolei?" I asked Grace.

"It's southwest of Pearl City," she answered. "It's a really nice area. People call Kapolei the second city of Oahu. It's its own city, but it's also technically part of the Honolulu City and County. It's a pretty wealthy area of town."

"I know it's not the Cloud storage lead," Biers said to me, "but how would you feel about checking this out?"

"Well, a lead is a lead," I said, though I really didn't want to go on another car ride with Biers any time soon. I mean, what were the chances that we'd end up with another dead body? "Let's go get this over with."

Chapter Six

GRACE WASN'T EXAGGERATING about how nice an area Kapolei was. We all rode in my car, since we couldn't fit comfortably in Grace's Jeep. It was about a thirty-minute ride, but we passed it without incident. No car chases for us this time. Biers and Rice chatted quietly amongst themselves in the backseat, and Grace stared out the window, lost in her own thoughts. I wondered if she was thinking about Jin Hamada.

The TomTom I always drove with led us to the house last listed as belonging to H. Graham—in this case, one Harold Graham. It was a nice home, sort of picturesque, looking like it could belong in those Thomas Kincaid paintings my grandfather used to like so much, complete with flower boxes hanging outside the two windows that faced the street and beautiful deep-red azalea bushes on either side of the stairs leading up to the wide porch. Yes, there was a small wooden swing on the porch.

"Anyone else feel suddenly more wholesome?" Grace asked.

"Not me," I replied. "This place makes me feel almost unclean in comparison."

"There's a joke in there somewhere. I'm just too lazy to find it."

"That's probably better for all of us."

Grace and I remained at the bottom of the steps while Biers and Rice rang the doorbell. It wasn't the old-fashioned "ding-dong" kind, but the one that let out an annoying buzzing sound.

Next to me, Grace shuddered a little. "You okay?"

"I'm fine," she answered stiffly. "That noise just sounds like the buzz that happens right before the doors locked closed on the cell block." Her sudden shift in demeanor made sense, then. She'd spent time in lockup when charged with Carrie's murder, and I imagine it stuck with her in a few ways that no one but Grace would ever fully know.

When the door opened, instead of an elderly person behind it, there was a young girl, mid-twenties. She had long auburn hair, bright eyes, and a heart-shaped face. She studied the four of us uncertainly—who could blame her, four strangers turning up on her porch? She relaxed the slightest bit when she saw Grace there, like the presence of another woman was somewhat comforting to her.

"Can I help you?"

Biers cleared his throat. "My name is Edwin Biers, and this is Daniel Rice. We're looking for the family of Harold Graham. We thought this was his home."

"It is. I'm Maggie, his granddaughter. What's this about?"

"That's a bit difficult to explain," Biers said, digging a photograph out of his pocket. "Can you tell us if one of these men is your grandfather?" Maggie took the photograph and studied it. I watched her face and saw no sign that she recognized anyone on it.

"Maggie, who's there?"

An older woman came shuffling toward the door behind Maggie, using a walker. She had wispy white hair and big glasses perched on her nose. She was skin and bones, her face wizened and lined. Despite the fact that she was using a walker, she moved with a confidence and strength that belied her obvious age.

"Oh, it's nothing, Grandma," Maggie said quickly. She started to pass the photo back to Biers, but the woman caught sight of it.

"Oh my word, what is that?"

Maggie sighed and passed the photo to her grandmother.

"Where on earth did you get this, Maggie?"

"These people gave it to me."

"I'm sorry if this is forward, but were you married to Harold Graham?" Biers asked, taking a step forward.

The woman suddenly blinked back tears. "Yes, I was."

"Does he happen to be one of the men in this picture?"

"Yes sir-ee, right here." The woman pointed to a man on the left end. He was handsome, his face still boyish, filling out his uniform nicely. "That's my Harold. These other men are from his original unit here at Fort Shafter. Where did you get this picture?"

"That's a bit of a long story," Rice said, stepping up next to Biers. "Do you mind if we come in for a few minutes?"

"Grandma," Maggie started, a warning in her tone. Clearly she didn't trust us.

"Sure," the woman said. "Come on in."

She led us inside to a sitting room. It was tastefully decorated, the sort of place that looked like it didn't see a lot of traffic. I imagined they reserved it for company, not everyday use. The woman, whose name was Janet, shuffled back to the kitchen, returning a few minutes later with a tray bearing six glasses of iced tea. Once they were distributed and she was comfortably situated in a winged-back chair facing the rest of us, Janet invited them to tell their story.

Rice and Biers took turns telling the story of their search and their discovery of the journal, the picture of H. Graham, and the mention of the treasure.

"Did you ever hear anything about a treasure or fortune stashed away?"

"Treasure?" Janet Graham laughed. "I think someone is pulling your chain, Mr. Biers. Harold never mentioned anything about a treasure."

"If I may ask," Grace said, lacing her fingers and resting them on her knees. "Where were you married, Mrs. Graham?"

Janet looked confused at the question. "Harold and I were married in West Virginia, where we're both from."

"What made you move to Oahu?"

I wanted to ask Grace where she was going with this line of questioning, but she'd been in the business longer than I had, and I trusted her instincts, so I just listened.

"It was always Harold's dream to get back to Hawaii after the war. Said he fell in love with the place while stationed here. We saved every day of our life to come here. Then, nine years ago, Harold up and took early retirement, and we were able to make the dream come true."

Biers and Rice exchanged looks at her words, and I had little doubt what they were thinking. I had to admit it wasn't unfeasible to think that maybe Harold wanted to return to the island to be close to the treasure he'd hidden—if he'd hidden it anywhere.

"Did your husband ever meet up with any of his old army buddies, Mrs. Graham?" I asked, not really believing that I was letting myself get caught up in all of this.

Janet looked like she didn't know why I'd be interested in this, but she humored me. "Once a year, yes, right up until two years ago."

"And what happened two years ago?" Grace inquired.

"My grandfather broke his hip," Maggie answered for Janet. "He never quite recovered from it, couldn't get out and about, certainly not to go camping. That's what he did with his old army friends. They went camping every summer."

Rice leaned forward eagerly at that. "Did they travel to different places for the camping, or does it always take place here on the island?"

"It's always been here on the island," Janet answered. "Harold would fly here to meet the boys before we moved here. The camping trip always lasted three days, every year around the middle of June. Harold always looked so forward to it."

"Do you happen to know where they went camping?" Biers tried not to let his excitement show, but he didn't succeed. Did he think that the camping spot was the location of the buried tontine?

Well, maybe it was. It would certainly make my life easier and bring an end to this mess.

"They always went to the same place in Nuuanu Valley Rainforest— though I can't tell you precisely where. I think Harold had a map, though. Hold on."

Janet left us there in the living room with Maggie, who waited until she was certain Janet was gone before rounding on us. "I don't know what you're up to with this fake treasure nonsense, and I don't know how you got that picture with my grandfather, but I'm not having it. My grandfather has been dead for three months, and I won't let you take advantage of her."

"We have no ill intentions toward your grandmother. We aren't asking for anything from her except for information." Biers probably thought he was being comforting, but Maggie's face made it clear she didn't buy a word of it.

"You watch yourselves," Maggie warned, eyes blazing. She obviously loved her grandmother very much, judging by the ferocity with which she defended her. It would be a very stupid mistake for us to cross this woman.

I took a deep drink of the iced tea Janet provided to hide my amused smirk at the way Biers shriveled up at Maggie's withering glare. It was nice to see that someone else found him about as charming as I did.

Janet returned with a folded-up map that looked like a tourist guide to the Nuuanu Valley Rainforest with an area circled. It wasn't too deep in, but it also didn't look like it was the sort of place one was allowed to camp. I couldn't see that doing much to deter men who were already involved in an illegal tontine that consisted of stolen goods.

"I'm pretty sure that's where they always went camping." Janet handed the map to Biers, who examined it like it was a pirate treasure map of some sort.

"Would it be all right with you if we take this?" Biers asked, gesturing with the map. "We could return it to you, but we'd like to check this place out."

"You can keep it," Janet said with a dismissive wave. "It was Harold's, and not something I really need to keep."

"Thank you for your time," Grace said, rising. She signaled for the rest of us to do so when we didn't immediately follow.

"No problem, of course," Janet said kindly.

"One last question," Rice said, ignoring the glares he received from both Grace and Maggie. "Can you give me the names of the men in this picture?"

Janet started to rattle off names, but Biers stopped her, offering her a pen and a notebook from his pocket. Janet wrote the names down, pausing to think of a few of them before finishing the list. "It's not everyone in that picture, but it's the ones that Harold would meet with. I hope this helps you."

"I'm sure it will, Mrs. Graham. Thank you so much."

Maggie and Janet walked us to the door, waving goodbyes as we returned to my car. Before I could even get the car door shut, though, Maggie came quickly toward us, glancing toward Janet at the door. She had a pleasant smile on her face, but it didn't touch her eyes.

"Did we forget something?" I asked politely, holding my door open.

"No, I just want to make one thing perfectly clear: don't come back here again."

"Sounds good to me."

IT WAS A long drive back to the office, with Biers and Rice speaking to each other rapidly in the back, their voices excited, their words rushed and almost fevered. As I thought, they zeroed in on the possibly conspicuous timing of Harold and Janet Graham's relocation to Oahu.

"Maybe the list got small enough that he wanted to be on the island when he won the thing," Biers suggested.

"That's what I was thinking! It definitely sounds like a pre-emptive move to me."

"Or," I added even though I knew I shouldn't—the sole voice of reason was rarely listened to—but I had to at least try. "It's possible he just really liked the island and when he finally saved up enough money, he decided to bring his wife here and give her a peaceful, tropical retirement paradise."

"Anything's possible," Rice said, as if *I'd* been the one with the more unlikely suggestion. "I say we go to the campsite and check it out!"

"What, now?" Grace chuckled, clearly joking.

Biers, though, nodded his head firmly. "Yes, now! No time like the present!"

"There's no way in hell," I said flatly.

"Gabe is right," Grace said, surprising me. "It'll take some time to get to Nuuanu Valley Rainforest, and then it'll take us time to find the campsite, even with the map. It's going to be dark soon, and the last thing we want is to be in the forest after dark."

Biers looked like he wanted to argue with us, but Rice just nodded reluctantly.

"Good. Why don't we meet up at the office first thing in the morning and get an early start heading out there? That way we can be sure that we have plenty of time."

"Fine. Let's meet at your office at nine sharp," Biers said. "*Sharp,*" he repeated, catching my eye in the rearview mirror. I didn't make a face back at him, but I really wanted to. I was trying to be professional, though, and so I just gave him a blank stare instead.

I'd never been so relieved to return to the office than I was the moment I pulled the car into the parking lot of Paradise Investigations. I didn't bother going back into the office or making small talk with Biers, Rice, or even Grace; I'd had enough of them for one day. For one week— for one year, even.

On my way home from the office, I stopped by the grocery store to stock up on food. I'd eaten out the last few nights, which allowed me to put off shopping, but Maka would likely be late tonight, and I was on my own for food, so I needed things.

I didn't have anything particular in mind, so I wandered the aisles somewhat aimlessly, picking up things that caught my interest. Sugary cereals, mini donuts, frozen toaster pastries, miniature pizza bagels, they all made their way into my cart, along with a twenty-four pack of Coke, a gallon of milk, butter, frozen French fries, and various meats, ranging from lunch meats to ground beef, pork chops, and spare ribs.

I was perfectly happy to call it at that, but I knew that Maka would have a cow if I didn't bring home some fruits and vegetables. I wandered into the produce section, musing about whether Maka would consider wine a fruit, when a familiar booming voice caught me off guard.

"Bruddah, I need choke pineapples. Like, as many as you got."

The words would have been confusing to me when I first arrived, but I'd come to learn about the pidgin language in use on the islands and didn't have any problem with that expression. The man needed a lot of pineapples. The pidgin originated from the eclectic mix of cultures on the island, where the native Hawaiians were forced to interact with English-speaking mainlanders, not to mention the varied Asian and Spanish immigrants that made their way there. With such a combination of languages and cultures, the pidgin developed as a way to communicate with each other, and had become a very real and prominent element of Hawaii.

The speaker was a big man, his head bald and glistening in the fluorescent lights of the grocery store. He stood in the fruits section, in front of a small display of pineapples, speaking to a store clerk who was at least a foot shorter than him and much narrower.

"Hiapo?" I called, pushing my cart up the aisle toward him, dodging past an older woman who walked with a stooped back pushing a cart full mostly of bananas and carrots.

Hiapo turned and looked at me, surprised. "Yo, Gabe, howzit, bruddah? You get any da kine?" I'd learned a while ago not to try to put any specific meaning to *da kine*; it meant pretty much anything you needed it to.

"You know," I said with a shrug. "An den?"

Hiapo broke out in a wide grin. "We gonna have you speakin' like a local bumbye. You gettin' there."

I smiled at the compliment. It wasn't true—far from it—but I appreciated the sentiment.

"We're pretty far from your lū'au place," I observed. Hiapo ran a nice private lū'au club near the beach, the sort that tourists didn't easily get invited to. Maka had taken me there to give me a real authentic lū'au experience shortly after we'd met.

"Places near me all ran out of pineapples—you believe it? You ever hear any kine like that?" Hiapo's shock and outrage were so real and so comical I laughed.

"Uh, how many pineapples do you need?" asked the store employee, drawing Hiapo's attention back to him.

"All dem." The man's eyes bugged out. "I'm makin' pork skewers, bruddah. I gotta have pineapples, ya feel?"

"But...but all of them?" The employee sputtered. "How many are you making?"

"'Bout five hundred. You like beef?"

Hiapo flexed threateningly, and while I hid laughter, the employee shook his head quickly. "I'll find out how many we have in the back." He scurried off to do that, Hiapo shaking his head as he watched him go.

"It's mad hard to find good help, ya feel?"

I nodded my agreement, still doing my best to swallow my laughter.

Hiapo turned a critical eye on my basket. "I appreciate ya dedication to meat, but where's the green, man?"

I shuffled my feet, embarrassed. "I was just getting to that."

Hiapo took it upon himself to help me in my veggie selection while waiting for his pineapple man to return. He explained the various ways I could use each one he picked up in its own dish or in tandem to be delicious. By the time he was finished, my other items were buried under greenery.

Thankfully the pineapple guy returned before Hiapo could load me down with spinach, which was where I drew the line.

"Good luck with your pork skewers," I called, beating a hasty exit to the checkout. I ended up spending more money than I wanted to—but that was always the case here, since everything cost more in Hawaii as most of it was imported.

I made it home and fixed myself a chicken Caesar salad since I had all the veggies for it, and settled in to watch bad television. By nine o'clock, I was ready to call it a day.

I had a quick shower and hopped into bed. Maka called me just as I was getting settled. I couldn't hold back a smile when I saw his number on the screen, along with the ridiculous picture he'd taken of himself with his hair crazily spiked with shampoo bubbles.

"I was just about to go to sleep," I said when I answered. "You've got great timing."

"I always do," he replied with a drawl. "And what are you doing going to bed at nine thirty? How old are you, sixty?"

"I've had a long and trying day," I said defensively. "I'll pull an all-nighter with you soon, just to show you how young I am."

"Ooh!" Maka's tone became suggestively anticipatory. "I look forward to it."

"You know what I meant." I kicked myself for the entirely unintentional innuendo.

"That's why I'm excited."

I sighed, deciding to give up the fight here for two reasons: one, I highly doubted I'd best Maka at this point, considering I'd given him too much ammunition; two, I didn't want my dick getting any ideas before I went to sleep.

"Night shift tonight?" I asked, changing the subject. I could hear the sound of the Honolulu police station in the background of the call: phones constantly ringing, people calling to each other, laughter, detained criminals shouting their innocence to their arresting officers.

"Yeah, til five." Maka sounded suddenly tired.

"Well, at least you've got some downtime. Which is a good thing," I added as an afterthought.

Maka chuckled, the deep bass sound going right through me to my cock. So much for my dick not getting ideas.

I heard someone shout Maka's name, though I couldn't recognize the voice—not that I would, since I didn't have many run-ins with Maka's coworkers. Well, I had my fair share, somehow, but not recently. At least not with homicide.

"I gotta go," Maka said quickly. "I just wanted to remind you—"

"Six thirty," I said, exasperated. He'd repeated it to me a million times to drill it into my head, and I'd suspected that the reminder partially motivated the call. "I remember."

"Good. Don't be late. Lateness is the one thing my mom gets really picky about. I'll try to call and remind you again tomorrow."

"I'm not a child, Maka," I huffed. "I'll remember, like I said."

"Good. Sleep well, babe." I noticed Maka didn't lower his voice when he shifted into those sorts of things, like Trevor used to do. He'd hated using pet names on the phone if he was anywhere anyone might possibly even have a chance of overhearing. I could imagine a police officer, especially a homicide detective, being uncomfortable displaying that sort of emotion at work, understandable in as machismo-filled an environment as a police station. Trevor, he was just a jackass.

"Have a good night, Maka. Be safe." It was my go-to sign off when he was working, considering how dangerous his job was.

We hung up, then, and I fell back onto the bed. Any thought I had of sleeping was now gone. All I could think about was the impending meeting with Maka's family, where I would no doubt fuck up royally. If anyone could find a way to do that, my history had proven it would be me.

Chapter Seven

I FELL ASLEEP eventually, only to be haunted by dreams of fucking up with Maka's family.

I was in Maka's family home, the home I'd seen featured in so many photos. Instead of being warm and friendly, like it looked in those photos and how Maka described it when he talked about his past, it was oppressive and foreboding.

Maka's family looked on at me with judgmental eyes, each of them finding six hundred ways I wasn't fit to be with Maka.

"He's a *haole*."

"He's too skinny."

"He doesn't know anything about Hawaii."

"He let himself get used by that idiot Trevor."

"He can't clean house."

"He can't even cook!"

"Look at his clothes—he has no style."

"Does he know how to surf?"

"I bet he can't dance."

The words kept coming and coming, until I ran out of the house only to find myself face-to-face with Maka and his mother. She was carrying a pig—an actual living, breathing pig.

"Where do you think you're going?" Maka's mother's words cracked at me like a whip.

"Uh, I was—I mean, I was just...uh—"

"Can the haole not speak?" Maka's mother asked him, like I wasn't standing there.

Maka shrugged, saying nothing to defend me.

"Well, if you can't speak, you can at least help me." The woman, her face a scowl, a polar opposite to the friendly, easy smile I'd seen in pictures, led me around to the back of the house. The backyard was impossibly huge, more woods than anything else. She led me to a round stump, about knee height, and twice that length around.

"What is it you need me to help with?" I asked, eager to please this woman.

She eyed me critically. "You trying to suck up, haole? I guess I can't blame you, since the moment I tell my boy here to dump you, he will."

Alarmed, I glanced at Maka, who nodded, to my horror. He would really dump me if his mother told him to.

"You got a job?"

I startled at the question, still looking nervously at Maka. "Yes. I, uh, I'm a private investigator."

Maka's mother let out a bark of laughter. "What kind of job is that? You sit in a car watching people cheat on their spouses? Disgusting."

I looked to Maka for help, but he studiously ignored me.

"You good in bed?"

"What? I don't think—"

"He's okay," Maka answered. "Not the worst I've ever had."

"*Maka!*" I couldn't believe he'd said that. I was *okay* in bed? What the hell?

"Could be worse, I guess. Here." She shoved a thick, hatchet-like tool into my hand.

"Uh, what is this for?"

"It's for killing the pig," she said matter-of-factly, like it was the most common thing in the world for her to ask me to do. "Get on with it; we've got lots of hungry people in there."

I stared at the pig as she placed it on top of the stump, looking at me expectantly. "What are you waiting for? Do it!"

I looked from the knife to the pig to Maka, unable to force myself to do as she asked and lift the knife. I'd never killed my own dinner before and didn't see how I could possibly do so now. The pig took advantage of my hesitation and scurried away, disappearing into the nearby stand of trees.

"Bah," Maka's mother spat, taking the knife from me. "He's useless, Maka. You don't need him. Let's go. Let the haole go back to where he belongs. You're better off without him."

Maka obeyed without hesitation, turning on his heel and marching off after his mother toward the house, leaving me standing there feeling devastated. "Maka? Maka, where are you going? Are you seriously leaving me? Maka? Maka!"

I JERKED AWAKE, nearly rolling out of my bed with the intensity of the motion. The dream lingered strong and powerful in my mind. I could still see the look of disappointment on Maka's face as he turned away from me, leaving me standing there like an idiot.

Except he didn't do that, I reminded myself. *It was a dream. Just a dream. Get a hold of yourself.*

I sat up slowly and looked at the clock on the bedside table. Seven fifty-nine. One minute before my alarm would go off and tell me I had to start getting ready to go to work. And less than twelve hours before I would face the judgment of Maka's family, and quite possibly a real chopping block.

I tried to put all that out of my head as I dressed and went through my morning routine. I scrambled a couple eggs and downed them, but I didn't really notice their taste. My mind was completely elsewhere, still lost in the fog of my dream.

Maka would never just turn his back on me, even if his family didn't like me. Which also wouldn't happen. Maka assured me they would like me. But how could he really know until they met me? What if they asked me to slaughter a pig? Even outside my dream, I don't think that's something I'd be able to do, though I'd sure as hell try, I guess. Anything to keep Maka.

These thoughts on constant loop in my brain, it was like I operated on autopilot. I barely remember the drive from home to Paradise Investigations. It couldn't be safe to drive in that state, but a man had to to go to work, right?

Grace was there when I pulled up at eight forty-seven, leaning against her Jeep and holding two Styrofoam cups of coffee. She was dressed like someone ready for a day of hiking: khaki shorts, a white tank top under a red-and-blue plaid short-sleeved button-down, her hair tied back in a tight ponytail and Timberland hiking boots on her feet. I gratefully took the one she offered me.

"You owe me nine bucks," she said when I'd taken my first sip.

I blanched, looking down at the cup. "Nine? For *this*?"

"Do you know how expensive coffee is after being imported?"

"The majority of America's coffee is grown here in Hawaii!" I cried.

"Yeah, but we export all of that and import this stuff." She raised her coffee in a toast. "To economics."

I returned the toast, muttering darkly.

At eight fifty-five on the dot Edwin Biers joined us in the parking lot. I was surprised to find him alone when he exited the car; Rice was nowhere to be seen.

Biers sounded pretty cheerful when he said, "Good morning!"

"When is Mr. Rice joining us?" I asked, resisting the urge to glance at my watch. They were the ones who were so firm about the time this morning, and now one of them wasn't here? Typical.

"He left me a message this morning saying he wouldn't be joining us." Was it just me, or did I really sense a hint of discomfort beneath Biers's words? Was it possible there was trouble in paradise?

"He's not coming?" Grace asked skeptically. "Why the hell not?"

Biers shrugged. "I can't say for sure; I haven't talked to him this morning. He mentioned having something he wanted to look into."

"Something more important than this?" Grace pressed, unconvinced. "That makes no sense. He was primed about this yesterday! Why would he suddenly have something better to do?"

"Because he thinks we're wasting our time," I said, studying Biers's face as I did. Based on the tiny flinch, I'd say he agreed with me. "Right, Mr. Biers?"

"Like I said, I can't say. He didn't say anything about that."

"But we can assume." I let out a long sigh. "Even your partner thinks we're off on a wild goose chase this morning. Great."

Grace threw a comforting arm around my shoulder. "Look at it this way: at least you get to see the Nuuanu Valley Rainforest."

"Always finding the silver lining," I said, but she was right. I'd been locked in the city since my arrival, and though I was getting out more than when I'd first arrived, when I spent weeks basically not leaving my condo, I still hadn't ventured outside the city and seen any of the beautiful nature sights the island had to offer.

Grace volunteered to drive, and I was more than willing to take her up on that offer. I didn't do well in traffic, and this time of day, I couldn't imagine there not being traffic. Plus, I didn't know the way and TomTom could only be relied on so much.

The morning drive was lovely, the sun coming in at the right angle to warm my face and arm but not be too intense on my eyes. Traffic wasn't great, and Grace guessed it would take about an hour to get there, and who knew how long to find the campsite, if it was even possible to do so.

"You know," said Grace, breaking nearly twenty minutes of beautiful, peaceful silence, "if you don't mind me saying, it seems to me like you're more invested in this whole venture than Mr. Rice."

"What makes you say that?" Biers asked in the tone of a man who'd thought the exact same thing and didn't want to admit it, maybe even to himself. "He's the one who came up with this whole plan! He put the group together, divided the work load, really spearheaded the whole effort."

"You don't find it odd that he did all that yet isn't here for what could be the big event?" I asked. I didn't particularly care to get involved, but there was something about asking the obvious questions that I loved. "Why isn't he here right now if he's spearheading this whole thing?"

Biers turned his head, looking out the window at nothing in particular. His meaning was clear: he didn't know what to say in response to my question, so he would say nothing.

Remembering my self-made promise to be nicer to him, I let it go.

Traffic thinned out a bit as we neared Nuuanu Valley Rainforest, and we picked up speed. We reached a parking area for the rainforest, paid the five-dollar fee—"That's going to be a work expense," Grace said, glancing at Biers—and parked.

The humidity was already intense when I slid out of the Jeep, and I regretted my long khaki pants and the dark-colored T-shirt I wore. What was I thinking?

"Judging by the map, we've got a bit of a walk ahead of us," I said, examining the map we'd received from Janet Graham. "That's assuming we find the place right away, which I'm not holding my breath for."

The map was deceptively simple, and I doubted it was to scale. There were probably hundreds of trails between the start of the trail and the campsite that would look like the right path but would only lead us in the wrong direction. I didn't trust myself to lead the way. I was well known to be terrible at directions, but I didn't feel confident about either of my companions, either.

"Did any of us bring a compass?" I asked, realizing the only thing I'd brought was a bottle of water. I prayed these two were better prepared than I was.

"I thought you two would take care of things like that," Biers said, eyes widening at the implication. "Didn't you?" I shook my head. We both turned to Grace, who had a smug look on her face.

"And they say men are the superior sex. I brought this." She dug into her pocket and brandished a beat-up, old compass.

"Are you sure this thing works?" I asked, taking it from her dubiously. It was dinged up and rusted and looked like it was one hundred years old, and I didn't think north was the direction the compass pointed. Not a comforting thought, that.

"At least I brought something." Grace snatched it out of my hands. "You two idiots showed up completely unprepared."

"You're right," I conceded, giving that she was. God, I hated admitting that.

"Then it looks like everyone is just going to have to rely on me today."

A shiver went down my spine. "We're going to die in this forest." I barely stepped out of Grace's reach as she took a not so carefully aimed swipe at my head.

Biers cleared his throat, eyeing us like a couple of misbehaving kids. "If you two are ready to act like professionals? We're burning daylight here."

NUUANU VALLEY RAINFOREST was beautiful. Everything seemed so much more vibrant. The leafy canopy had gaps that allowed beams of sunlight to speckle the path, dust motes and pollen dancing amongst the beams. Tree roots branched out into the path every now and then, interrupting the dirt path. The sounds of wild birds could be heard in the distance, their various calls echoing through the dome of branches and leaves. It felt almost surreal, as if I'd stepped into a painting.

We followed the path carefully, watching for places it might fork off as we went. The tourist crowd wasn't out in too much force, maybe because it was a Friday morning and they just hadn't reached the island yet. Whatever the reason, I was glad we had the trail mostly to ourselves. This way, when we ducked off the main trail, we wouldn't look suspicious.

"I think this is it," Grace said after about an hour of trekking through the trees. She pointed toward a trail that didn't look well traveled; if it hadn't been for some disturbed plants, I'd never have noticed it at all.

"What makes you say that?" I asked, craning my neck to see up the path, but it curled up ahead, blocking my sight. "Why is this one different than any of the ones we've already passed?"

"I just think it is," Grace said, confident for no reason I could see. "The other paths didn't look big enough for a group of people to go down, but this one does."

"I say we check it out," Biers said, wiping sweat from his forehead with the back of his hand. "We'll never find the camp if we just stay on this trail."

I nodded in acquiescence, since it was two against one. It was a valid point, anyway. We had to start venturing off the path eventually.

Brushing along the path, I was grateful for the long pants. I didn't know if poison ivy grew in the rainforest, and I didn't actually know how to recognize it if it did, but the pants would make it something I didn't need to worry about.

Biers stumbled over roots and things the uneven ground, studying the map. "It looks like the camp is to the northeast from the main trail. Are we going northeast?"

Grace checked her compass. "Uh, I don't think so right now, but the trail keeps winding, so who knows?"

"I'm going to repeat my earlier assertion that we're going to die here," I said, instinctively reaching out to steady Edwin before he could topple completely over after tripping over another root.

"You're such a pessimist," Grace called back to me over her shoulder. "But if you think we're going the wrong way, then we must be going in the right direction."

I sniffed. "Rude."

The path continued to twist and turn, making it difficult to tell what direction we were going. I just followed along, content not to be the one in the lead when we didn't end up in the right place.

We walked the trail for nearly an hour before Grace sighed and came to a stop.

I heard Biers mutter, "Oh thank god," under his breath and allowed myself the smallest of smirks. It felt good to me that the man who was the reason we were there in the first place wasn't enjoying himself. I used to be quite active back in Seattle—albeit with much less humidity and even less sun, considering Seattle spent most of its time under the cover of clouds—and was happy to see I wasn't that out of shape. I'd barely touched my water bottle, and though I was sweating, I wasn't feeling tired or too out of breath.

Biers, on the other hand, looked like he was on his last leg. His face was puffy and red, the front of his shirt plastered to his chest. His water bottle was less than half full, even this early into the day. Thinking of the time, I checked my watch. Nearly one in the afternoon.

"What should we do now?" Grace asked, turning around to face me and Biers.

"A rest might not be a bad idea," Biers wheezed.

"We're on a bit of a tight schedule, here," I reminded Biers. "Once it starts getting dark, we're out of luck. The sooner we find this camp the better."

"What I meant is do we turn back or keep going on this path?" Grace clarified.

The idea of wasting the entire day wandering down a single wrong path wasn't appealing, but there really wasn't any way for us to know how far off the main trail the location used by Harold Graham and his army buddies was.

I opened my mouth to say we should give it another half hour before we turned back when a sound caught my attention: voices, coming from somewhere off to our right. Someone was out and about nearby. An uneasy knot grew in the pit of my stomach. We were too far from the beaten path for it to be a coincidence.

Grace and Biers caught the same noises. Their bodies tensed and they looked around for the source. I waved my hands, catching their attention, and pointed to the right. We took the moment to go off the beaten path, pushing carefully through the underbrush and foliage as we sought out the voices. My bad feeling grew as we continued. I pressed ahead a bit, not letting Grace take the lead. The gentleman in me, I guess.

We walked through the trees for a good five minutes before I caught sight of movement ahead. About ten yards ahead there was a man dressed all in black with sunshades on his face, walking around what looked like a clearing.

The campsite? I crouched down, searching for a better opening in the trees through which I could see the clearing. From my vantage point close to the ground, I picked out at least three more pairs of legs walking by. The ground was turned over, like someone had been digging. From what I could tell, the clearing was wide and roughly circular in shape, like the area circled on Harold Graham's map.

I had no doubt we'd found the campsite.

Grace shuffled her way up next to me, leaning over to whisper, "Do those men look familiar?"

"Yeah, unfortunately," I replied. At least one of them was from the coffee shop. "Are they following us?"

"If they were following us, they'd be behind us," Biers said from my other side, startling me.

"Good point," said Grace. "Do you think that's the campsite?"

"I'd bet a lot of money on it," I said. The presence of these men troubled me. How did they know about the campsite? We'd only learned about it the previous day. How far ahead of us were these guys, and how?

"What do we do now?" I asked.

"We should go back to the car, maybe come back tomorrow," Grace suggested.

"No!" Biers all but shouted. I tried to cover his mouth shut him up, but he reared back out of my reach. "We've come too far to go back now! What if..."

"Hey! Did you hear that?"

The blood froze in my veins. The question came from one of the men in the campsite, and I had no doubt Biers was what he was referring to. Maybe if we stayed perfectly still the men wouldn't notice us.

"It came from over here," the man continued. I heard approaching boots on the leaf-strewn ground.

"Go, go, go," I hissed, scrambling backward and urging Grace and Biers to turn around too. I rolled over and to my feet, not worrying about staying unseen since the guy was going to find us anyway.

I heard Grace and Biers right behind me as we crashed through the underbrush, but it was hard to tell if anyone was directly behind us.

"We shouldn't go to the main trail," Grace called up to me. "It will be too easy to find us. Turn south and stay in the trees!"

I didn't see what it mattered, since all we needed to do was outrun, but then I heard the unmistakable sound of gunfire somewhere behind us. The trees and the echo made it hard to tell if it was close, but I had to assume it was. Suddenly Grace's plan had a lot more merit.

I moved in the direction I assume was south, dodging between trees and shrubbery and hoping I was going the right way. I glanced back to make sure Grace and Biers were still behind me and nearly stumbled into a thick blanket of bushes that stretched on for a good bit.

Grace and Biers both came to a stop behind me, winded and faces sweaty. With them no longer moving, the sound of pursuit was clear.

"Why did we stop?" Grace asked, the slightest hint of fear in her words. "Stopping seems like a bad idea."

"I have a plan," I said, gesturing toward the bushes. "Why don't we hide there in the bushes? They're thick, and if we crawl in, we should be covered."

"I'm about on my last leg, so I'll go with the plan that involves us no longer running." Biers spoke between deep, ragged breaths.

There wasn't a lot of time to argue about it, so we agreed, dropping to the warm, packed-dirt ground before crawling into the bushes. Luckily none of them seemed to be sporting thorns or anything that could scratch us, aside from a stray branch.

The ground beneath the bushes was cool in contrast, the dirt untouched by the heat of the sun an almost pleasant sensation against my face. I kept my breathing shallow so as not to inhale too much of it, but choking to death didn't present the most imminent danger at the moment.

I heard Grace or Biers shifting positions somewhere in the brush, rustling leaves and making far too much noise, and I bit my lower lip to keep from calling out for them to just stay still. At this point, we'd made our own beds, and now had no choice but to lie in them—literally.

All I could do was lie there, counting my erratic, panicked heartbeats while praying this wasn't the end of the line for me. I'd never really thought of myself as someone with a lot to live for before, but now I did. I was starting to really love my life in Hawaii. I had a boyfriend, a job that gave me freedom, and I was living in one of the most beautiful places on the planet. I wasn't ready for that to end just yet.

Please, I prayed, *please let us get out of this. I don't want to die in this stupid rainforest.*

The minutes ticked by agonizingly slowly. I couldn't see the sky, and I certainly wasn't going to move or look at my cell phone to find out what time it was. I occupied my time listening to the forest around us for any sign of the men who were following us.

I didn't want to get my hopes up, but it was beginning to look like we'd lost them. The sounds I'd heard earlier were gone; all I heard was the squawking and chirping of birds, the rustle of the leafy canopy in the wind, and the sounds of my own breathing.

Were we safe? Had we gotten away? I wanted to be sure before I stuck my head up out of the trenches. Maybe the men were lying in wait, hoping for us to stick our heads up. I would stay there hugging the earth however long it took to be certain—well as certain as it was possible to be.

I lay there until I couldn't stand it anymore and then crawled on my belly out of the bushes. It felt odd to be in a standing position again after so much time on my stomach; for a moment, I felt dizzy, having straightened too fast. Grace and Biers followed me out, Grace seeming mostly composed and Biers looking like an anxious mouse.

"Think it's safe?" Grace asked me. It was a rather stupid question, I thought irritably, since I wouldn't have come out if I didn't. I refrained from saying so, though; I just nodded tersely.

"We need to get out of here," Biers said urgently.

"For once, Mr. Biers, you and I are in complete agreement on something."

We found the main trail and made our way to the Jeep without any more problems. Once in the safety of the Jeep, I dug my phone out of my dirty pocket and saw I had a missed call and a text message from Maka.

Don't forget: 6:30.

According to my phone, it was already pushing five o'clock. It would take us an hour to get back. I'd still have time to shower and get ready. But there was something else on my mind just then.

"How did those guys know?" Biers burst out before I could. "How the fuck did they know about the campsite?"

"That's what I'd like to know," I said grimly. But I was starting to have an idea.

"Maybe they paid a visit to Janet and Maggie after we did," Grace suggested.

"How many maps do you think the man had?" Biers scoffed.

"There's only one way I can think of," I said. Before I could share my theory, Biers's phone rang.

"Hello? No. Something happened. I'll tell you about it in person. Meet us at the office. We'll be there in forty minutes." He hung up and turned to us. "That was Daniel. He'll meet us at the office."

"So we gathered," said Grace, giving me a dark look. I could see she and I were thinking the same thing. Biers, well he'd find out soon enough.

WE REACHED PARADISE Investigations at forty-five minutes past five. Rice was waiting for us when we did.

"What happened?" he asked before we could even get out of the Jeep.

"We'll talk about it inside," I said before Biers could start in. Biers gave me a strange look, but said nothing.

"Okay," Rice said once we were inside. "What happened? You're starting to really worry me."

"I bet," I muttered, not taking my eyes off him.

Biers explained everything while Grace and I watched Rice carefully. The progression from interest to shock and then horror on Rice's face seemed genuine enough, but I wasn't going to easily take that at face value; for all I knew, Rice was a damn good actor.

"I don't understand; how did they know?" Rice asked when Biers was finished.

"I was hoping you could tell us," I said pointedly.

Rice blinked. "I don't follow you."

"I think you do." I crossed my arms over my chest. Biers looked between us, confused, but I paid him no attention. My focus remained on Rice.

"If you've got something to say, just come right out and say it," Rice snapped, drawing himself to his full but not so impressive height.

"What were you doing earlier today?" Grace asked, her tone less confrontational than mine but her eyes just as cold. "Why didn't you join us on the way to the campsite?"

"You were gung ho about it yesterday," I added.

"I didn't think there was any need for all of us to be there, that's all. Besides, I doubted the tontine would be there, and I figured I could be of more use at the library, doing research."

"Conveniently nowhere around when the men were at the camp. That's a little coincidental, don't you think?"

"What about the other times?" Grace added. "What about Alvin Liu? You were M.I.A. then, too, weren't you? And when Mr. Biers here was at the coffee shop?"

"You're saying I had something to do with this? You think I hired those men or something?" Rice turned to Biers. "Edwin, you don't believe this, do you?"

Edwin looked uncertain for a moment, and then his resolve hardened. "No. Of course I don't. And if either of *you*," he rounded on

Grace and me at that, "had bothered to ask me before you accused Daniel of this, I would have told you the exact same thing then."

"Somehow these guys have had information that would seem impossible for them to have randomly," I stressed for Biers. Could the man really be this stupid? "How could these people have known Alvin Liu was connected to your hunt for the treasure? How could they have known where the campsite was? Only the four of us were there, and we didn't even have a solid idea where it was!"

"The people were following me," Biers started.

"Did you visit Alvin Liu before you went there with us?"

"No, I didn't, but—"

I was picking up steam as I went, all my frustration circling this case rising to the surface and fueling my words. I heard the incremental increases in my volume, but could do nothing to stop it.

"And there was no way they could have overheard us in that house when we were talking to Janet Graham. And even if they somehow found a way to do that—"

"Even if they did, they wouldn't have known the location of the campsite," Grace finished for me before I was shouting at the top of my lungs.

"There's got to be some way they did that," Biers said firmly. "Daniel would never hurt Alvin, and he would never send these men around. Why should he? He knew where the site was, and it wasn't like we were keeping him from it. He's got nothing to gain by doing this."

I took a deep breath in preparation of telling Edwin Biers how much of an idiot he was when I realized it had gotten dark in the office while we were standing there.

"Fuck! What time is it? *Fuck.*" Grace looked wildly around, so I just grabbed my cell phone. Six-twenty-two.

"Fuck me!"

I was late, and I was dead.

Chapter Eight

I LEFT PARADISE Investigations right then, without a word. I jumped into my car and sped out of the parking lot so fast I was surprised my tires didn't squeal. The twisted knot I'd felt in my stomach this morning was back with a vengeance. Compared to everything that had gone wrong today, this was much worse.

I was fifteen minutes from home when my cell phone rang. I didn't need to look at it to know it was Maka. I punched the button on my steering wheel that activated the speakerphone in the car.

"Maka, I'm—"

"Where the hell are you?"

I cringed; I'd never heard so much anger in Maka's voice, and it wasn't directed at a criminal, it was directed at me. "I've been waiting at your place for an hour!"

"I'm sorry, it's just that I didn't realize what time it was," I stammered. The sound of a horn startled me, and I almost swerved into the neighboring lane, but managed to maintain control of the car. That was a miracle, considering how much I was shaking.

"I told you what time we needed to be there! I texted you. I tried to call you earlier, and you didn't pick up."

"It's this job, and something just came up—it's complicated, but I can tell you about it later."

"You don't know how to use a phone? My mom went to a lot of trouble with dinner tonight because I told her you were coming. She called me this afternoon to verify, Gabe, and I told her you'd be there, one hundred percent."

"I..." I fell silent, unable to find my voice for a moment. "I know I should have called, but I wasn't really in a position where I could. If you'll just let me explain—I'll be home in like ten minutes, and I'll be ready to go." I remembered then that I was covered in dirt. "Actually, I'll have to take a shower, and then I'll be good to go. You'll understand when you see me. It's a crazy story."

"When I see you? What, you think I'm still at your place? I'm already almost to my parents' house."

"Oh, okay." My voice sounded like it had gone up an octave. "I'll, uh, okay. Why don't you give me the address, and I'll hurry there as soon as I finish showering?" I brought the car to a stop at a red light, tapping the wheel anxiously with my thumb. Why the hell didn't the light realize I had somewhere important to be?

"I told you how my mom feels about people being late. Don't bother."

The words felt like a physical blow, but even worse was the tone of disappointment in his voice. "Maka, I'm sorry, this case has been pretty crazy..."

"I know. I know you have a demanding job—I do too. But this was important to me, and you know that. If you didn't want to come, you should have just said so in the first place. Now I have to show up without you and explain to my family why you aren't there even though I told them you would be."

"Maka, I'm sorry."

"I'm here. I gotta go."

Maka ended the call, my car speaker's making a clicking noise that cut right to my heart.

I couldn't make myself stop shaking, and I had to keep blinking to fight back the tears that burned my eyes, blurring my vision. A heavy lump had formed in my throat, and it was a miracle I could breathe. I'd fucked up, big time.

I DID WHAT I always used to do when I had a problem: I called Grace. I didn't trust myself to drive with the distraction of talking to Grace, so I waited until I got home. I explained what happened as best I could— which might not have been that well, considering the state I was in. I didn't even remember what I said. Whatever it was did the trick, though, because twenty minutes later, Grace was at my door, two bottles of wine in hand.

"Thought you might be able to use these," she said, hefting the bottles in emphasis.

"Thanks, Grace." I let her into the condo and started to close the door behind her, but not before my eyes fell on Maka's empty parking spot. A pang of something shot through me—grief, regret, guilt, a mix of the three—and I turned away quickly, closing the door with a lot snap.

"Maka was pretty pissed, huh?" Grace asked.

In the brief time since I'd let her in, she'd somehow fetched two wineglasses from the kitchen and was busy popping the cork on the first bottle—a red of some kind; I didn't bother reading the label. The cork made a satisfying *pop* and came free. Grace sat it aside and poured two liberal glasses.

"To say the least." I sat down on the couch and took the glass she offered me. I gulped about half of it down without even tasting it. "I can't blame him. He reminded me what time it would be happening again and again. It was my fault for not paying attention to the time with everything going on."

"Is it possible you wanted to miss the dinner?" Grace asked me delicately. I looked up to find her surveying me over the rim of her wineglass.

"What's that supposed to mean?" I asked hotly.

"Well, you've been dreading it ever since he brought it up, right?" Grace prodded. I knew the look on her face; she was about to switch into her "tough love best friend" mode. That never ended well for me; it was basically an excuse for Grace to yell at me in a way that made me the bad guy if I responded in kind. The only way to deal with it was to head her off.

"Okay, I admit it. I didn't really want to go. But I was going because I said I would—honestly," I added, seeing the disbelieving look on Grace's face. "Today the time really got away from me. We *were* getting shot at, remember?"

Grace nodded to concede my point. "Why didn't you want to go?"

I squirmed for a moment. "I mean, meeting the parents—that's a huge step, right?"

"Does it have to be?" Grace asked.

"Of course it does! Meeting the parents when I know how much they mean to Maka? It's got to be important. He even said it was. I don't know if I'm ready for such a big step in that direction."

Grace cocked her head to the side, like a curious boxer. "In what direction?"

"That's a major sign of commitment, and I don't...I don't know if I'm ready to make it so official." Just the thought of it had me gulping down the rest of my wine and reaching for the bottle.

"Are you not sure you want to be with Maka?"

"That's not what I said."

"Then I'm confused." Grace put her wineglass down and leaned forward, propping her elbows on her legs. "What's the problem?"

She was asking me to answer a question that I didn't think I could. "The problem is the last time I was so...*official*, or what have you, was with Trevor, and look how that turned out! It hasn't been that long. I don't want to rush into anything this time. What if I mess up again?"

"Again?" A fire lit in Grace's eyes at that. "You didn't mess anything up, Gabriel Maxfield. Trevor was a complete bastard and was the one in the wrong—not you. *Not you.* It's about time you got that through your head."

"It's hard for me to see it that way," I muttered, staring down at the floor between my feet.

She didn't understand what it was like, how Trevor made me feel. Anything that ever went wrong in our relationship—which, in hindsight, was pretty much everything—ended up being my fault because Trevor would twist reality to fit his preferred narrative, and I believed him. You didn't just shake that off right away. Even though he'd stolen from me and treated me like crap, I still felt like I was responsible for things falling apart sometimes. How did you explain that to someone who'd never felt it before?

"I know," Grace said at last, her voice gentling. "But you have to realize Maka isn't Trevor. The standards of behavior are completely different."

"I do know that, but knowing something on an intellectual level and knowing it on an emotional level are very different." I slumped down on the couch, genuinely distraught. "I think I fucked things up forever."

Grace took my hand and squeezed it. "Probably not forever, Gabe. Just talk to him."

"I'm pretty sure he doesn't want to talk to me," I said dryly.

"Well you have a good excuse now," Grace pointed out. My expression must have been blank, because she sighed and said, "The guys in the forest, remember?"

"You think *I* should be the one to tell him? Why don't you do it?"

"I feel like there's two things that need to get taken care of tomorrow: the police need to be told about the guys shooting at us in the forest, and someone needs to check in with Jin to see if he's made in progress."

There was no mistaking the slight blush that came over her cheeks right then. "And let me guess: you'd rather take care of Jin."

"If you don't mind."

I did mind, a little bit, because the idea of talking to Maka terrified me in the wake of the argument. He was furious—and I couldn't blame him, honestly.

I thought about it for a moment. *Had* I purposefully sabotaged today? If I'd been more careful about watching the clock...but I'd been occupied with the job we were working.

A job you didn't even want, a treacherous voice in my head reminded me.

"I know what will you make you feel better," Grace said, patting my leg. "Let's order Indian-Thai fusion and watch *The West Wing*."

Okay, she did know me. We were best friends for a reason, I guess.

I SLEPT FITFULLY that night, waking up every hour or so. I was intensely aware of the closeness of Maka's home. He was just on the other side of my living room wall, but he might as well have been back on the mainland for all the distance I felt between us in those moments.

I woke up for the final time at ten past seven and decided I wouldn't be able to get back to sleep, and it was now or never when it came to talking to Maka.

I forced myself out of bed, pulled on sweatpants and an old T-shirt, and hurried out the door to Maka's condo. I didn't even pause to slip on shoes. It was cloudy outside, the sky gunmetal-gray, and the air carried the scent of promised rain. It was October, so the temperature was fairly cool in the mornings, and as I stood in front of Maka's door, I regretted not putting on the shoes.

I debated what I would do. Given the circumstances, did I knock on the door instead of using my key? I didn't know the rules when it came to us being angry at each other, since it was the first time it had happened to us.

I settled for ringing the doorbell. When he didn't come, I hesitantly opened the door with my key and peeked inside. The place was quiet, all the lights off. Damn it, he'd already gone to work. The last thing I wanted to do was trek to the police station to talk to him. It would be awkward talking about personal things there, and I hated the way things were left. Also, I didn't want to look desperate, following him to work after we had a fight.

Didn't look like I had much of a choice, though, so I returned home, showered, dressed, and grabbed a banana to eat on my way to the Honolulu Police Station.

The building where Maka worked was an old structure, the walls white concrete. The words Honolulu Police Station were mounted over the door in bronze letters. The American flag hung from one corner of the entryway, the Hawaiian flag from the other. Even this early in the morning, the place was a flurry of activity outside.

I'd visited Maka there one time before, shortly after I'd heard that Ashford, the slimeball who'd tried to kill me, was beginning his trial. I knew he worked on the third floor, so I made my way there.

The homicide bullpen was filled with detectives looking like they'd all just gotten in for the morning. Most of them had coffee; a few still had their jackets on. I spotted Maka's partner Benet and frowned. I wanted to avoid him at all costs. I already knew Benet didn't like me; I didn't want to give him more reason to.

"What are you doing here?"

I nearly jumped out of my skin, wheeling around to find Maka standing there, his face impassive, looking at me like an acquaintance and not his boyfriend.

"I came to talk to you," I said nervously. Now that I was here, facing him, my heart wouldn't stop racing, and it wasn't because of him startling me. "I stopped by your place this morning, but you weren't there. Obviously."

"Only twelve hours late," Maka said acidly. "I'm busy." Maka skirted past me, starting for the bullpen.

Now that I was here, though, I wasn't going to give up, no matter how much I didn't want to have this conversation with him in this particular place. I followed right behind him.

"I wanted to talk to you about yesterday—I wanted to say I'm sorry. There's no excuse for—"

"I don't want to talk about it," Maka said firmly. He dropped into his seat at his desk across from Benet, who looked at me like I was something unpleasant that had been tracked in on the carpet.

"Trouble in paradise?"

"Well, I do," I said, ignoring Benet. "I should have been honest with you and told you the idea of meeting your family made me nervous, but I didn't. I'm sorry. That doesn't mean I intentionally didn't show up, but maybe subconsciously it had something to do with it."

Maka's face didn't change at all. "I told you I didn't want to talk about it here. I'm at work. Unless you have something related to work, we can talk later."

"Okay, fine." I planted my hands firmly on my hips. "How's this for work-related, huh? I was shot at yesterday."

Maka sat there, staring at me, unblinking. Benet straightened suddenly, eyes narrowing. "That's a hell of a thing to say."

I turned the full-force of my glower on Benet, appalled at the implication I would lie to get Maka's attention. "It's a hell of a thing to have happen, too."

"Where?" Maka asked, his voice all business. "When?"

"Yesterday afternoon at the Nuuanu Valley Rainforest," I said.

Maka's eye twitched. "Was anyone hurt?" I might have been reading into it more than I should have, seeing only what I wanted to, but it almost looked like he was adding *were* you *hurt* with his eyes.

"No. Well, not that I know of. But—"

I fell silent when Maka and Benet leapt to their feet. Benet reluctantly put down a bagel and brushed his hands together to clear them of crumbs.

"We'll talk later," Maka said, marching past me, Benet on his tail.

"But, Maka," I called.

"Later!" he called back, not turning back to look at me.

Chapter Nine

"How did it go?" Grace asked me as soon as I walked through the doors of Paradise Investigations. She was sitting at Hayley's desk, the file marked "Biers Case" open next to the computer and her comically oversized coffee mug on the other side.

"I'll let you know when I know," I answered. "Where's Hayley?"

In response to my question, Grace reached over the Biers file to the telephone at the edge of the desk and hit a button on it.

Hayley's voice filled the room from the answering machine. "Hey, this is Hayley. I really wanted to thank you for the time off you've given me this week. It's made me realize how much I like not being there. Sorry to do this over voicemail, but I didn't want to go back. Hope you find a new secretary soon! Oh, and I hope I can count on you for a positive reference." The answering machine cut off with a click.

"Do you think we should read anything into the fact that she doesn't like being around us?" I asked, crossing behind the desk to see what Grace was working on.

"What? Like, a personal failing on our part? No way; if anything, it says something bad about *her*."

I chuckled. "What are you doing?"

"Got the background check back on Biers," Grace replied, pointing to the new information she'd added to the file.

I picked it up and glanced through it, not that it took long; there was basically nothing in there. "So he's clean."

"Pure as the driven snow," Grace agreed.

"Having lived in Washington, how can you use that saying?" I asked, putting the background check back in the file. "You know how dirty that snow got after people were driving on it."

"I don't think that's what they mean by driven."

I shrugged, starting toward my office in the back. "Did you get anything good from Jin Hamada?"

"He hasn't gotten back in touch with me," Grace said, shouting even though I was just behind her. "I left him a voicemail, though."

I sighed. "Okay, so what's the next step?"

Grace wheeled the chair around to face me. "I called Biers and had him give me a list of names for all of the people involved in this whole tontine business."

"Without socials, we can't do background checks," I reminded her. "Besides, it would cost a fortune."

"No, but we can do Google searches. I want to see if what Rice said is holding up, about the others ending up dead, too."

I groaned. "Do you seriously want us to start scanning obituaries?"

Grace smiled at me. "Here's your half of the list."

I craned my head to see the other piece of paper she had. It looked quite a bit shorter than the paper I had. "Why do I have most of the names?"

"Because I got the background check."

"You just opened the envelope!"

"I'm also still trying to get a hold of Jin and see if he accessed the Cloud server yet."

"What, not going to pull the girl card on me?"

Grace narrowed her eyes at me. "I'm going to choose to ignore that." She turned the chair around as huffily as one could manage to do that. I rolled my eyes and walked into my office. I kept the door open in case she wanted to yell in to me, which she probably would, knowing her. Grace didn't focus well, so she'd get bored and try to talk to me about something.

In the meantime, I sat behind my desk and logged into my computer. I opened Google Chrome and hopped right into a Google search for the first name on my list: Terrance Parker from Chicago, Illinois. I had to try multiple combinations before I got anything substantive. It was a hit to a Chicago newspaper—specifically an obituary.

"I hate when I'm right," I muttered, reading through the obit. Terrance Parker, forty-two, died in a car accident when his brakes failed at a busy intersection.

I typed in the next three names, Vivian Franks from Walnut Springs, Texas, Tolly Rainard from Los Angeles, and Patrick Harris from Knoxville, Tennessee. All three of them came up in obituaries from various causes—Vivian killed in a hit-and-run while walking to the nearby grocery store, Patrick from falling off his roof while fixing torn shingles, and Tolly, like we'd heard from Rice when we first met him.

The information was freaking me out.

"Gabe," Grace called, and something in her voice told me she'd started learning something like what I'd gotten.

I walked out into the front room. Grace was looking at the screen at a headline from a paper in Tallahassee, Florida: "Elderly Woman Dies in House Fire." The article had a picture of a woman with cotton-ball hair and cat-covered shirt. Beneath it was "Clare Redding, sixty-four."

"Let me guess, not the first death you've come across?"

"The third," Grace said grimly.

"All four I checked were the same. It looks like every person involved with this tontine search is dead."

Grace drew a line through the three names on her list, and then Alvin Liu's at the bottom. I looked at mine. There were three more names on it, and I gave them to Grace one by one. Exactly the same—each one had somehow died within the last year.

"Someone's killed them all, and no one's noticed?" Grace asked incredulously.

"They all live in different states," I pointed out. "There wasn't any central connection to be made, except Biers and Rice."

"Well, we know which one *wasn't* being shot at yesterday," Grace said. "So I have an idea where I'd put my money."

"Whoever did it must be trying to make sure they're the only ones who know about the tontine," I said, squeezing the back of the chair and rocking back and forth on my heels. "That means we're going to be targets now, because we know about it."

"Maybe I shouldn't have recommended you move to Hawaii, Gabe. It seems like I get guns pointed at me a lot more frequently when you're around."

As much as I wanted to, I couldn't argue with her on that.

I was spared having to by Biers's arrival. The poor guy came into the office looking like he hadn't had a wink of sleep. Dark circles surrounded his eyes, his hair stood on end, and his face had taken on a pallor that made me think of someone with the flu. He seemed, if possible, even more twitchy than he'd been before.

"Sorry I'm late. I wanted to take a roundabout way here, in case someone was following me." Yup, the man's paranoia remained intact.

"Earlier you asked me for a list of the people involved in the hunt. What was that for?"

"We just wanted to do some routine research on everyone," I said, glancing at Grace while trying to think about how we should present it. "It's normal in an investigation like this. It helps if we know as much as we can."

"And did you find anything important?"

"You said you'd lost contact with all of your friends, right? Obviously you know about Alvin Liu. We'd heard about your friend Tolly's death in a car accident—well, it didn't take us too long to find that—I'm sorry, I don't know how to put this any other way—they're all dead. Aside from you and Daniel Rice, every person whose name you gave us is dead, all within the last year."

Biers looked like his legs were going to come out from under him. I quickly helped him to the couch, Grace following behind us.

"I knew something terrible had happened," Biers murmured to himself. "How did they die?"

"Various ways," I said, thinking it better not to go into the specifics. "But all of them were accidents—or at least made to look that way. Given what we've experienced here and what happened to Mr. Liu, I think it's safe to say I believe your conspiracy theory, Mr. Biers. Someone has taken out all the members of your tontine hunt."

"What...what does this mean?" Biers asked, face even whiter than it had been.

"It means you really are in danger. Someone who knew about this hunt is trying to kill everyone else involved."

"Someone..." Biers's brow furrowed. "You think Daniel is behind this?"

"He was the one in Los Angeles," Grace pointed out.

"Not to mention he was nowhere to be found when we discovered Alvin Liu's body, or when we were in the rainforest."

"He was the only other person who knows, right?"

"We can't say that for certain," Biers said, standing up and patting his palms against his thighs in what might have been a nervous twitch. "Maybe one of the others said something, or they were hacked."

"Mr. Biers," I said, tone making it clear how ridiculous I found that idea.

Biers deflated a bit, returning to the couch. "Maybe you're right. This is insane! I can't believe Daniel would do this."

"We can't really know a person that easily online," Grace said gently, rubbing her palm on Biers's back in a small circle. "The faces we wear online can easily be masks—no matter how long you know someone. I mean, look at catfishing. Some people carry out years-long relationships with people over the internet, never knowing that the person they were speaking to wasn't who they thought they were. It's so easy to lie through the computer."

"Let's just keep focusing on the tontine," I said, fighting the urge to run my hands through my hair. It already looked messy enough; I didn't need to make it worse. "The best way to keep ourselves safe is to bring this damn thing to an end already. If we hand the tontine over, there's no reason for someone to try to kill us. In this case, anyway."

"That means we need to find out what's in that Cloud drive," Grace said, marching back to Hayley's desk—well, what was formerly Hayley's desk—and grabbing her cell phone. She dialed Jin's number and stood there, one hand on her hip, the other holding the phone to her ear. Her posture, expression, tension, and the set of her jaw all told me she was incredibly nervous, maybe making her way into being genuinely afraid at this point.

"He's still not answering." Grace bit her lower lip. "He's never not with his cell phone; it's an important part of his job."

"Guys," I asked slowly, an unfortunate idea dawning on me. "Does Rice know about Jin and the Cloud server?"

Biers's eyes widened with horror. "Yes. I told him about it."

Grace was across the room and in Biers's face in two steps. "How could you do that?"

"Daniel has been involved with this the whole time," Biers said defensively, taking a step back from Grace and ending up on his ass on the couch. "I didn't know that he might—that, well you know." He waved his hand vaguely.

"We need to get to Jin, fast."

NONE OF US knew how to get to Jin Hamada's place, but since he operated as his own LLC, we looked up his business license and found his address through that. We were lucky he didn't use a PO Box to register, or we'd be screwed. Grace drove there, speeding like a maniac. She drove almost as fast as Biers had during the high-speed chase.

Jin's place was a first floor, one-bedroom apartment not terribly far from Paradise Investigations. It was a nice apartment complex, the sort of place where you had to enter into a courtyard to get to the apartment doors. Once the three of us were in the courtyard, it wasn't hard to figure out which one was Jin's, even without the numbers nicely placed above each door. Jin's was the one with the door broken in.

"Oh god."

Before I could stop her, Grace was heading toward Jin's apartment at a run. I let out an exasperated noise and followed her. I probably would have done the same thing if it was Maka's apartment door hanging open at a precarious angle like that.

I hesitated at the door before finally stepping inside. Directly ahead was a hallway that led back to a bathroom and a bedroom. To my right was the kitchenette area—a stovetop and a beat-up looking microwave, but a pristine white refrigerator—and to my left the living room area. The living room must have been where Jin did all his work, because while it did have a couch and a television crammed into one corner of the room, the majority of it was taken up by a large L-shaped desk that was pretty much covered with computer tech. Three monitors and as many keyboards. Well, used to be, anyway.

The desk was a mess. Every single electronic device on it had been smashed to pieces, with broken glass from the screens, plastic, chips, and wires all over the place. A rolling desk chair was knocked over and thrown aside.

"Jin?" Grace called, panicking. She hurried toward the back of the apartment, opening the bedroom and bathroom doors while calling Jin's name. "He's not here," she said, voice quivering, eyes wild.

"Good lord," Biers said from the doorway. "Please tell me there's not a dead body here."

"No body," I said, looking around. "But that raises an important question: where is Jin?"

"What if...what if whoever did this kidnapped him?"

"They didn't bother keeping Alvin Liu alive, so why would they kidnap Jin?" I asked, confused. It didn't make a whole lot of sense.

"Who kidnapped me?"

Biers, Grace, and I screamed, turning around fast to find none other than Jin Hamada standing in the doorway of the apartment, looking genuinely perplexed.

"Woah, woah! Calm down, dudes. Why would someone kidnap me? And what are you doing in my—oh, *kusso!*" Jin swore in Japanese, spotting the mess on the table.

"I didn't do it!" I said quickly, throwing my hands up to show I had nothing with which to cause the destruction of what was probably thousands of dollars of property.

"We just got here," Grace added. "We thought you were dead and came over here to make sure you weren't dead."

The confusion returned full-force to Jin's face. "Wait. Will someone please explain what's going on?"

Grace and I explained what we'd learned about everyone who worked on the tontine ending up dead.

"Dude, this is pretty crazy," Jin said when we finished. "If I'd been home, do you think I'd be dead right now?"

"Probably," I said, not wanting to lie to him. I didn't know for sure, of course, but after the others and Alvin Liu, I had to guess it was more likely than not.

"Why weren't you here, anyway?" Grace asked, voice hyper-nonchalant. "Were you on a date?"

I boggled at her utter lack of subtlety. "Who goes on dates at ten in the morning?"

"It could happen."

"I have breakfast with my mom every Saturday," Jin answered, either oblivious to Grace's ridiculous digging or choosing to ignore it to be kind to her. I thought it was the latter.

"Aw," Grace cooed, smiling warmly. "That's so sweet."

Jin smiled shyly. "Since my dad died, she's been kind of lonely, so I do my best to see her as much as I can. I get busy during the week, though, so Saturday mornings are reserved for her."

"Is everything all right in there, Mr. Hamada?" An older woman, walking with the use of one of those canes with four prongs on the bottom instead of just the one, poked her head in the door. She pronounced Hamada like a combination of the word ham and the ending of lemonade. She had blue-rinsed hair set in meticulous curls, wore a pink Gucci jogging suit, and had pink Nike tennis shoes on.

"It's okay, Mrs. Neidermeyer. Just had a bit of an incident."

"I was on my way back from a job fair when I saw these three goons run into your apartment and called the police," she informed him, scowling in the direction of Grace, Biers, and me. "You ought to be ashamed of yourselves, causing trouble for a sweet young man like Mr. Hamada here."

Grace took a step toward the woman—Mrs. Neidermeyer, according to Jin. "No, no, we didn't have anything to do with—"

Grace had to jump back to avoid a blow from Mrs. Neidermeyer's cane. The old lady swung it with a surprising amount of force.

"Oh no you don't, you hussy. Don't try to sweet talk me! I saw you come in here when Mr. Hamada wasn't home!"

"Hussy?" Grace repeated furiously. Before she could get into a fistfight with a cane-wielding senior citizen, though, Jin went to the rescue. Someone needed to, and I sure as hell wasn't going to do it. I had to admit watching Grace get whacked with Mrs. Neidermeyer's cane would give me a certain amount of satisfaction.

"Calm down, Mrs. Neidermeyer," Jin said, voice calm and gentle. "These three didn't do it. I work with them."

Mrs. Neidermeyer narrowed her eyes suspiciously, like she didn't quite trust that Grace could work with Jin. "You mean she's not a sweet-talking hussy?"

"No, ma'am, she's not," Jin assured her, though I'm sure I detected the hint of a smothered laugh in his words.

"Okay then, if you say so." Mrs. Neidermeyer narrowed her eyes at Grace. "I'm watching you."

She hobbled away then. I watched her go, thinking she probably didn't need that cane anywhere near as much as she pretended. Probably just a handy makeshift weapon to have around.

One that could destroy computers easily.

Jesus Christ, Gabe. You're sitting here thinking a little old lady destroyed Jin's apartment and is in on a conspiracy to kill you. You're starting to sound as bad as Biers. The fact that Biers was right had very little bearing. He was right, but he sounded crazy.

"So now what?" Grace asked after making a face at the departing Mrs. Neidermeyer.

"Now we wait for the police." *And pray it isn't Maka that responds.*

THANKFULLY SINCE NO one died Maka didn't respond to the call. The police that did come looked like they wanted to be doing anything but responding to a simple property destruction case. They asked a battery of questions—was anything stolen? Did he have any enemies? Did he have any idea why someone wanted to destroy his stuff? Was he involved in anything untoward on his computers?—and then left to file their report and let the crime scene techs come in and get to work.

When that happened, we departed his apartment, knowing he wouldn't be able to return there for several hours while the techs worked. With Grace driving and me in the backseat with Biers now that Jin was with us, we set off.

I assumed we were on our way to the office so we could talk about what was going on, but instead we ended up pulling into the very busy parking lot of a sprawling four-story shopping center near the ocean.

"Uh, Grace, what are we doing?"

"This is the Ala Moana Center," she told me, maneuvering the Jeep into a parking space.

"I can see that it's a shopping center," I said impatiently, "but what are we doing here?"

Grace turned the Jeep off and removed the keys from the ignition. "Well, the way I see it is this: someone is probably following us and trying to kill us because we know about the tontine and they want to keep it all for themselves. Fair?"

Jin, Biers, and I nodded.

"Well, if we go back to Paradise Investigations, we'll be alone, just the four of us, and an easy target. Besides, whoever this is probably expects us to go back there, since we work there. I think we're safer if we stay in a more public place. It would also be harder for us to be overheard here, if someone *did* follow us."

"Are you sure you don't just want to go shopping on Biers's dime?"

We made our way casually to the food court. We each split up to seek out our favorite foods: Biers got fried chicken, Jin got McDonald's, Grace got Korean food, and I got a massive order of French fries. We found a table surrounded by big groups. It would give whoever was following us—if they still were—no place near us to sit, and they were loud. To one side, we had a family of six, clearly on vacation and arguing with each other, to the other a group of seven high school kids, and the other two tables were filled with adults just out and about—one table coming complete with a crying baby.

Once situated with our lunches, Biers jumped right into his questions. "So, did you find out anything?"

"Jesus, Biers, let the man at least eat his lunch before we start hitting him with the questions," I reproached.

"It's cool, it's cool," Jin said, taking a massive bite of his hamburger. When he spoke again, it was through a mouthful of food. "I can multitask." I was grateful he decided to swallow his food before he went on. "The Cloud server had a lot of personal files—music, some letters to the editor-type things he was writing, photos, games—he was a big gamer, really liked *Total War*. Even played *Shogun*, which is definitely the best in the series—"

"Anything relevant to the thing?" Biers interrupted.

"Oh. I'm not sure. He had a document that just referenced some old-school pirate named Po'okela. I haven't been able to find any real information about him on the internet, though."

I saw Biers's disappointment before he hid it behind a giant crispy chicken thigh. He was obviously hoping for more from the Cloud drive—especially since it was enough that Alvin Liu got killed and Jin's stuff got wrecked.

"So now we figure out the next step," said Grace, setting aside her now empty bibimbap bowl. She was a fast eater. "We should try to find out something about this Po'okela guy."

"I think we're forgetting something really important," I said, dipping a fry in one of the little paper cups of mayonnaise and then the ketchup. I paused before putting the fry in my mouth because I noticed Jin and Biers were looking at me like I was crazy. "Are you guys looking at me this way because you want to know what we're forgetting or because I'm eating mayonnaise on my fries?"

"Mayonnaise," they said together.

I ignored them, chomping into the fry. Some people just didn't know something delicious when they saw it.

"What we're forgetting," I continued, "is Daniel Rice. What do we do about him?"

Jin's face darkened. "The fucker owes me seven thousand dollars!"

"I'll pay to cover the cost of repairs," Biers told him. "You never should have been caught up in this mess. It happened because you were working on my case, so I will cover the damages if insurance doesn't."

"I think we need to turn Rice into the police," I announced. Biers looked at me like I'd grown a second head. "Why is that such a crazy idea?"

"We'd have no choice but to tell the police about the tontine in that case," Biers said. "All of this—and everyone's deaths—it would be meaningless. I'm not ready to do that yet."

"Will you be ready when you end up dead?" I snapped. Realizing we were in public and people could hear us, I lowered my voice. "Are you that set on this treasure that you're willing to endanger not only your life, but mine, Grace's, and Jin's as well? Isn't it enough that everyone you were friends with on this thing lost their lives?"

Biers's face reddened as if I'd struck him. "What exactly would you propose we tell the police, then? You didn't believe me when I told you all of this the day we met, did you?"

"No," I conceded.

"And we have no actual evidence to support our theory that Daniel is behind this," Biers went on. "Just because we're convinced doesn't mean the police will be. All that's going to happen if you go to the police is we'll lose the tontine and Daniel will flee. At least if we keep pursuing it, there's a chance we can actually come across some evidence incriminating Daniel."

"Fine," I conceded. "But the next time someone points a gun at me or destroys something or threatens anyone in connection to this case, I'm going to call my boyfriend without hesitation." Well, I'd call the police; I didn't know if Maka would be so open to taking my call.

"Agreed," Biers said without hesitation.

"We still have to decide what to do about him," Grace said, eyeing my French fries hungrily. I pulled my plate closer to me to protect them.

"Why don't we do a sort of false flag operation?" Jin suggested. "Feed him bad information?"

"That is a brilliant idea," I said, smacking Grace's hand away from my French fries. "If we can throw him off the trail that will give us time to find this thing, give it back to the Japanese government, and get him arrested for extra measure."

"So we stay focused on the tontine, then." Grace gave up on my fries and turned her focus to Jin's; he shared them with her willingly. *Foolish man*, I thought. *You have no idea what you've started with such a simple gesture.* Grace was like a vampire of your food. Once you invite her into your plate, you can never uninvite her.

"Which means finding out who this Po'okela was," Biers added. "If there's nothing on the internet, we might have to start relying on the natives and locals. Someone who would know a lot about the history of Hawaii."

I thought about it for a moment, drawing a blank, and then it struck me as obvious what we needed to do next.

"I know exactly who we should talk to," I said, grinning.

Chapter Ten

HIAPO MET US at Waikiki Beach. I felt bad for involving him in this, considering people who got involved ended up dead or hurt, it seemed, but we needed answers, and from what I'd learned in conversations with Hiapo, and according to Maka, Hiapo was very well versed in Hawaiian history and lore. He felt it was his duty, preserving the culture of the islands and its people. A noble goal, I thought. Definitely better than being a private eye.

Biers's eyes bugged out of his head a little bit when he saw Hiapo, but that tended to happen when people first met him, due to his size. He was an intimidating-looking man, but in the time I'd come to know him, I knew he was an utterly gentle soul who would not wish harm on someone if they set him on fire.

"Aloha, bruddah," Hiapo said, greeting me with a tight hug. "Who are your friends, here?"

I introduced them, and Hiapo gave them each a friendly "Howzit?"

"So, what did you need? Sounded kinda urgent on the phone."

"We're looking for information about a guy called Po'okela. He was a pirate, supposedly."

Hiapo's eyes widened at the name. "Yeah, Po'okela was a pirate in service of the first Kamehameha. Not a lot of people know his name, though. How'd you come by it?"

"Research," I said before anyone else could chime in. The last thing I wanted was to put Hiapo in even more danger by telling him what this was about. Maybe if he didn't know about the tontine he wouldn't be in any real danger. It was a long shot, for sure, but it was the best shot we had. "Do you know much about this guy?"

"Yeah, of course. Po'okela was one badass brother, from the stories. He served King Kamehameha, acting basically as his navy. Before that, though, he was a ruthless pirate. According to the story, he was arrested and brought before Kamehameha when he was still just a kahuna and was given the choice of exile at sea or serving the man. Po'okela listened to kahuna Kamehameha lay out his vision for a unified Hawaii. He was so moved by it that he pledged himself into service to the kahuna and swore to see him become king."

"So he gave up pirating?" Jin asked.

Hiapo snorted. "Nah. He might have believed in Kamehameha's vision, but he was still who he was deep down. He just stopped pirating any place that was loyal to the kahuna. His raids served to weaken the morale and the defenses of the people who resisted unification."

"What did he do with his treasure from all of his raids?" Biers asked, clearly captivated by the story of a pirate. Did he see himself in a similar light? Did he imagine himself a modern-day pirate, but in reverse, returning the goods that were stolen?

"He gave three-fourths of it to the kahuna, but kept a fourth of it for himself, as was his agreement with Kamehameha. Obviously nobody is one hundred percent sure, but they say there's an island right here off the coast of Oahu where he stashed his treasure."

Grace frowned. "There aren't any islands off the coast of Oahu."

Hiapo gave her a condescending look. "Of course there are. There are dozens of tiny islands off the coasts of the big islands, they just too small or unimportant to put on the maps. Most of 'em aren't even a mile around."

"Thanks a lot for your help, Hiapo," I said, feeling like we'd gotten enough information from him. How much of it was useful remained to be seen; who knew if this Po'okela guy even existed, and if he did, his reputation might have been overexaggerated in order to strike fear into the rival kahunas. The small mass of land where he'd hidden his treasure, though, that was promising, and it might have served as inspiration for Harold Graham and his fellow tontine members, true story or not.

"Anytime, bruddah. But Gabe, wait just a minute. I wanna ask you a serious question man. Personal, you know?"

I glanced at Grace and she nodded. "Jin, Mr. Biers, let's wait in the Jeep. Gabe will only be a minute."

I mouthed *Thank you* to her and waited until they were out of earshot before giving Hiapo my undivided attention.

"What is it you wanted to ask?"

"Everything cool with you and Maka? I saw him yesterday, and he didn't seem that great. Kinda pissy."

I knew that's what he was going to ask.

"Actually we are having an issue or two," I started, explaining to him what had gone down.

"*Ohana's* important to a man like Maka," Hiapo said sagely. "More important than his job, more important than just about anything else. It's part of being Hawai'ian."

"I get that," I said, kicking the sand in front of me in frustration. "I really do get it, Hiapo, and I know I fucked up. I feel really bad, because it was so important to him and I just got scared. I think I wanted to miss it, you know, on some level. But that was a mistake, and I know that now. I'm ready for that with Maka. I'm ready for whatever Maka's ready for."

"'Cause you love him," Hiapo said.

"I do. A lot. It's been a month, but I do. I think I did the moment I met him, you know? It's corny, yeah, but it's also kind of true. Something in me resonated with him." I felt stupid just saying it, but it was how I felt, and I needed to be honest with Hiapo so I could be honest with myself. "Do you believe in destiny, Hiapo?"

"*Uhane hoa*," Hiapo said, almost like a prayer. "Soul mates. Yes, I believe the moment we lay eyes on our *uhane hoa*, some part of us knows it. I think that's what you felt when you saw Maka for the first time—the parts of you that are soul mates recognized each other."

"Wow," I said after a moment, my heart tight in my chest. "That was deep, Hiapo."

"I'm going to help you," he announced, a determined look on his face. "Love is on the line, and the bond of *uhane hoa* must be protected."

I chuckled, a bittersweet feeling taking over me. "I wish I knew how."

"Actually," Hiapo said, a small smile on his face that grew wider as he spoke, "I think I have a good idea."

I DIDN'T REALLY notice the ride back to the office, instead thinking about Hiapo's plan for fixing things between Maka and me. It was sound enough, but would it work? I didn't know, and wouldn't until I finally talked to Maka. I barely said goodbye to Jin when we dropped him back off at his apartment. I caught the briefest bits and pieces of Grace and Biers's conversation and forgot it almost immediately after. It just didn't seem important, until I heard Grace curse under her breath.

I looked up, surprised we were in the parking lot of the office. It took me a moment to realize why she swore: Daniel Rice's car was parked there right next to the main door. In a spot reserved for handicapped parking, no less.

"What do we do?" I asked Grace.

"Don't let him know we're on to him or he might get spooked," Biers whispered, though he didn't need to, since there was no way Rice could hear us from inside his own car. "We've got to be careful and feed him just the right misinformation so he believes us."

"If we keep it simple it shouldn't be a problem, then," I said. "Seriously—simple, guys. If we say too much or get too complex, it's easier to figure out the lie. Just tell him we don't have any real leads, or give him one fake one."

"What should the fake lead be?" Biers asked, leaning between the seats to converse with Grace and I more comfortably.

"Something that will keep him distracted for a few days," said Grace. "Something involving traveling, maybe."

"Guys, we're going to look weird just sitting in the Jeep," I muttered, opening the door and sliding out before Rice grew any more suspicious than he probably already was. As I exited the Jeep Rice followed suit, a tired look on his face.

"I hope you all had better luck today than I did," he said as I slid my key into the deadbolt and turned it, pushing the office doors open. The inside was cooler than the outside thanks to the shades being drawn, but not by much. I went to the thermostat and turned the central air on.

"Depends on what you define as better luck," Biers said with a strangled laugh. I gently hit my head on the wall beside the thermostat. If Rice knew Biers as well as they said they knew each other, then he'd notice something was up if Biers kept acting this way. Would Rice just kill us all when he found out we were on to him?

"I spent all day trying to find *something*, but I had no idea what I was even looking for." Rice flopped down on the sofa with a sigh. "Even if I'd seen something useful, I couldn't say for sure that I'd have known what it was. For all I know, I saw the answer and ignored it."

"That's certainly possible," Biers said, sitting down next to Rice on the couch—not as close as he might have before this morning. "We knew this would be difficult, though."

"So, did you?" Rice pressed.

Biers squirmed. "Did we what?"

"Have more luck than I did?"

"Oh. Uh—" Biers caught my eye and I gave him a subtle nod, thinking *He's going to blow it*. "Yes, we did. I think, maybe. We've come to the conclusion that the spot had to be somewhere within easy distance from Fort Shafter—what with their deadlines to be back on base and all. They couldn't have been too far from the place at any given time while in service. The place *must* be around there somewhere."

Rice didn't look convinced. "I thought we'd ruled it out."

"We had, but looking at it...it just makes no sense to rule it out. They wouldn't have had easy access to transportation, not that could get them too far from the base. It's got to be out there."

Rice's brow furrowed as he thought about it. "I guess that makes sense. We can look at maps and get an idea what's out there."

"Maybe the library will have good reference maps to compare back then and now," Biers suggested, doing a pretty good job of mimicking his old level of excitement. Unless, of course, he'd convinced himself this might actually be true.

"We can get there tomorrow and—damn it." Rice's face fell. "The library is closed on Sunday. We'll have to wait until Monday to get any work done."

Biers patted his shoulder consolingly. "It's waited since the end of the war, it can wait a little longer."

Rice nodded, resigned. "You're right, of course."

"Good. If that's everything we need to talk about tonight, I'm going home. We should all take tomorrow off—it's Sunday, after all, and there's nothing urgent to do tomorrow. We deserve a day off, don't you think?"

"Agreed," Grace said, throwing her arm across my shoulder. "I think we've worked really hard the past four days. Besides, I'm kind of ready to not see your faces for twenty-four hours."

"Hear, hear!" I wasted no time, hurrying for the door. "You can lock up behind yourself, right?"

"Sure," Grace called behind me, sounding a little annoyed. "Glad to be of help!"

I opted to ignore the blatant sarcasm.

The drive home had me thinking about Hiapo's plan to fix things with Maka again. The more I thought about it, the more certain I was that it would work. *If* I could get Maka to agree to it. That required talking to him, and I hadn't quite worked up the courage to do so since our conversation at the police station. Every time I thought I'd gotten the courage to do it I couldn't bring myself to hit "Call."

After four times of picking up the phone only to set it back down on the table, I jumped to my feet and made my way to the bathroom. I turned the bathroom sink onto ice-cold and splashed my face several times, in hopes it would help me get a fucking grip.

"I can do this," I said, staring at myself in the mirror, water dripping from the tip of my nose and my chin. "It's just Maka. That's all. I'm just calling Maka like I've done a hundred times before."

I returned to the living room, grabbed the phone, and called Maka. The urge to hang up was overwhelming, but I resisted, my thumb hovering over the button. I was so busy fighting that weaker part of me I didn't realize the phone was no longer ringing; Maka had answered.

"Hello?" Maka's voice came again, sounding as if he was repeating himself. "Gabe?"

"Yeah, I'm here—sorry. I'm here."

There was an awkward beat of silence before Maka spoke. "Well?"

"Well what?"

"You called *me*, remember?"

Oh, yeah. Shit. *This is going great.* "Right. I was hoping you'd agree to meet me for lunch tomorrow. I know I don't deserve it, but I'd like a chance to apologize—really apologize for Friday."

"I'm working tomorrow afternoon," Maka replied, voice gruff. My heart sank, and I realized Hiapo's plan wasn't going to work after all. Before my hopes were dashed completely, though, Maka seemed to take pity on me. "I'll be home by five-thirty. I'll go to your place around six."

"Okay, six. Sounds good. I'll be waiting."

"Okay. Bye." There was something in Maka's voice, a hurt that let me know this wasn't easy on him, either. Our relationship had become an important bedrock for both of us, and to be so distant was like being kept away from home.

But tomorrow evening I'd fix it. I called Hiapo as soon as I was off the phone with Maka.

"Phase one complete."

Chapter Eleven

I SLEPT IN Sunday morning for the first time in ages. Normally I would have been woken up by Maka or Grace asking me if I wanted to have a surfing lesson. Grace was probably doing her own sleeping in, though, and Maka didn't seem to be in the mood to offer me a surfing lesson today.

I had a lot of pent-up, nervous energy coursing through me, and I didn't really know what to do with it. I tried to settle in and watch some Netflix, catch up on all the shows I'd missed, but I simply couldn't stay focused even through one episode of *Luke Cage*. Every time I checked my phone, it seemed like time hadn't moved even the tiniest bit. How could it be eleven-thirty when I checked my watch thirty minutes ago and it was eleven-thirty then? Maybe I'd broken time itself.

I tried napping. I tried cooking. Nothing worked. Finally I gave in and turned to the less pleasant side of being an adult: laundry and cleaning. Having clean clothes and a clean place to live was great, of course, but it was less great when you were the one who had to make sure it got that way. Kids just didn't know how good they had it until it was too late.

I started the laundry first and then turned my attention to deep-scrubbing the kitchen. I wasn't a messy person, but the deep-down cleaning that was necessary every week or so was a pain in the ass, and I hated doing it. The kitchen took until just after noon, and around that time, Hiapo called me to confirm the plan was a go and everything was going to be in place on time.

After that, I moved on to the bedroom—changed the sheets, opened the windows to air it out a bit, and reluctantly started in on the bathroom, pausing only to take the laundry from the washing machine and put it in the dryer.

I was scrubbing the toilet bowl, both hands encased in thick rubber cleaning gloves, when I heard my cell phone ring in the living room. I tried to use the rim of the toilet to push myself up, but it was still slick with cleaner and the rubber glove kept slipping. It took me three tries to get to my feet. I rushed to the living room, trying to get the rubber gloves off. They were both slick with water and cleaner, so I couldn't get the grip I needed to get them free. My phone was face down on the couch so I had no idea who was calling me, and I couldn't answer with cleaner-covered gloves on my hands.

What if it was Maka calling to cancel? What if it was Hiapo calling to tell me that something had gone wrong with the plan?

Why can't I get the stupid gloves off?

I finally managed to work one free and grabbed the phone, but it was only Grace. Feeling like I'd rushed for nothing, I answered.

"I'm not going to work," I told her as soon as I hit Accept.

"Wow, hello to you, too," she said. I could practically see her scowl through the phone. "Someone woke up on the wrong side of the bed this morning."

I felt bad for being so snippy with her. It wasn't like she was purposefully going out of her way to make my life miserable. "Sorry, Gracie. I'm not trying to be a bitch. It's just that it seems like this whole Biers and Rice treasure hunt has taken over my life, and I don't want that. It's already messed things up for me and Maka."

"True enough," Grace conceded, and I knew all was forgiven. "I actually wasn't going to talk to you about work at all. There's a beer garden downtown that's having a great sale tonight, so I was thinking about hitting it up and wanted to see if you wanted to come with me. It'll be fun. We haven't been out-out together in forever. Basically since college."

"I'd love to," I started, and Grace groaned before I could even finish. "What?"

"I know that voice. That's your *I don't want to go, but I'm trying to be nice about it* voice. Just be honest if you don't want to go. You're a grown man and can do whatever you like. I'm not unreasonable. God."

"Okay, it's not that I don't want to go, Grace, it's that I don't want to go *tonight*."

"What happened to getting out and about?" Grace exploded in true, predictable fashion. "I thought you were ready to participate in life instead of staying locked up in that condo of yours."

"And I thought you were reasonable," I fired back. "I'm not hiding in my room. I *am* ready to get out there—just not tonight."

"No time like the present, Gabriel."

I wished I could reach through the phone and strangle her, but luckily for her, I couldn't. "Not. Tonight. Grace." I said, letting my annoyance show. "I'm actually genuinely busy. I have plans. With Maka."

I visualized the lightbulb of understanding flickering on above her head. "Oh. *Ooh.* I see. Okay, then, good luck. Message me and let me know how it goes. I'll have wine on the ready just in case."

"Thanks for the confidence," I said dryly, hanging up on her.

I went back to work cleaning the bathroom, finishing the toilet and moving on to the shower and then the sink and then the tile floor. By the time I finished with that it was already after five. I smelled like bleach and toilet cleaner. I couldn't imagine that being appealing to Maka, so I'd have to take a shower before he got here.

I cringed a bit at the thought of taking a shower in the freshly cleaned bathroom, but that was life. We cleaned things just to get them dirty again, an endless cycle that we perpetuated.

Time seemed to crawl by even slower after my shower—allowing me to change clothes at least four times, as per usual—until at last Maka rang the doorbell. He was dressed in the clothes he'd worn to work, I guessed, and his expression was placid but distant.

"Aloha," I said, feeling an awkwardness that never used to exist between us. "How was work today?"

"Fine," he said a bit stiffly. "Am I coming in, or...?"

"I thought we'd go out for dinner." I grabbed my car keys from where they hung by the door. "Nowhere special or fancy, but I don't have anything to cook with here." It was a lie, since I'd just gone shopping, but Maka didn't know that.

I feared Maka would turn me down—and reading his face I could see he was considering it—but finally he shrugged.

"Okay, sure."

We got into my car, and I turned onto the road toward the beach. "I see you're not using the navigation," Maka nodded toward my TomTom, which had a black screen.

"I'm starting to learn my way around," I said, happy he'd noticed. His tone was still cool and almost formal, but it was better than it was the day before.

"I want you to understand why I'm upset," Maka said suddenly, and any happy feeling I had vanished like so much smoke.

"I know it was important to you," I said quickly, needing him to know that I got it. "*Ohana* is important."

"It's more than just *ohana*, Gabe. That *is* part of it, and it's a big one, but not the biggest. I wanted you to meet my family, and that's not something I've ever done before. I've never brought a guy home to meet them. It was my way of showing you how important *you* are to me, how important this relationship is, and where I stand in it. I'm upset because I thought we were in the same place, but I don't think we are."

That damn knot was back in my stomach and tighter than ever. His words sounded like the sort of thing you said to someone when you were breaking up with them.

Oh god, is he going to break up with me?

"I can see how you got that impression," I said, hoping that my rising panic didn't come through in my voice. "But you're wrong. I hope you let me prove it to you."

Maka turned and peered out at the passing city, giving a noncommittal grunt.

Okay, Hiapo, I thought, feeling Maka slip away from me, *this better work.*

MAKA REALIZED WHERE we were going when I turned into the mostly empty parking lot. "What are we doing here?"

"This is the first place we ever had a meal together," I reminded him. "We got lunch after confronting Delgado about Carrie's death. It was from a food truck right there." I pointed to the place the truck had been parked.

"I remember," Maka said softly, like he was surprised I remembered. "The trucks are gone for the day, though, so where are we going to eat?"

"Don't you worry. I've got it all taken care of." I gave him my best mysterious smile and got out of the car, Maka following suit. The nights were growing cooler, the only real sign the seasons were changing in Hawaii. The parking lot was higher up than the shoreline, and a line of palm trees obscured the beach to the southeast.

As we walked along the sand, I caught sight of the lights flickering ahead, unmistakably firelight.

"What's that?" Maka asked suspiciously, noticing it as well.

"I don't know. Let's check it out." I didn't look at him because I knew if I did he would know I was lying.

It was mostly dark, the city lights to our right, the ocean, moonlight glittering off its waves, to our left. As we rounded a bend, we saw the source of the firelight.

I couldn't hold back a gasp of surprise.

Ten collapsible tables and chairs were set up, surrounded by at least thirty lit tiki torches. A buffet set-up reminiscent of Hiapo's lū'au place was toward the city side, and Hiapo stood behind it with a wide grin visible even across the space between us.

He'd exceeded expectations.

"There they are!" A cheer went up from the twenty or so people at the tables. A woman no taller than five feet came toward us, holding her arms out welcomingly, a beautiful lei around her neck.

Maka embraced her, still looking confused. "Mom? What are you doing here?" He looked back and forth between his mother and me. "Did you do this?"

"Not alone," I said, gesturing toward Hiapo behind the buffet table. "I had a little help. Listen, I know what you said in the car. This is my way of trying to show you that despite what you think, we *are* in the same place, Maka. I was scared of that at first, after Trevor, but there's nothing for fear but facing it, right?"

I turned to Maka's mother. "Mrs. Kekoa? I'm Gabriel Maxfield. You can call me Gabe. Nice to meet you."

Maka's mother threw her arms around me, pulling me into a tight embrace. "Please, call me Lana. It's so good to finally meet you."

Without another word, she took my hand and led me toward the table where two women sat with a man who I could tell immediately was Maka's father. He was basically an older version of his son, though his muscles had gone to a paunch somewhat, and his hair was starting to recede from the front of his head. He was where Maka got his twinkling eyes and quick, ready smile.

I looked back at Maka, who just shrugged, amusement on his face.

"Everyone, this is Gabe, who Maka's been constantly talking about." Lana introduced me to the two women, Maka's aunts—his father's sisters—and his father himself, Kapa'a. They all greeted me warmly.

Maka started to sit down next to me at the table, but Lana stopped him. "Maka, go get the boy some food, okay? He looks hungry."

"I can do it myself," I said gently, starting to rise, but Lana pushed me back into my seat.

"He can do it himself," Maka protested.

"Go on. Don't argue with me." She shooed him away and turned to me. "I don't know where his manners go sometimes."

Hiapo provided a great evening, with a near-magical atmosphere and incredible food. I sat next to Maka, talking to his parents and other relatives who wandered over to meet me. My reputation preceded me, apparently.

At some point during the evening, Maka's hand came to rest casually on my leg just above my knee. It was a simple gesture made while talking to his father about sports or something, I wasn't listening, but it made my heart swell like the Grinch on Christmas Day.

I finally got the feeling we would be okay.

I excused myself and went to the bathroom near where the food trucks parked during the day. A dark sedan moved slowly through the parking lot as I walked by, and I tensed. Had whoever Rice hired followed me here? Had I put Maka's family in danger?

Shortly after, the car pulled into an empty spot and a couple got out, making their way for the beach, hands already all over each other. Just a couple out for a moonlit stroll. I was starting to be as paranoid as Biers.

On the way out of the bathroom, I lamented the lack of paper towels for my hands. I hated resorting to wiping my hands on my clothes, but there wasn't much else I could do.

I was so focused on my hands that I didn't notice anyone behind me until a hand grabbed my shoulder and pulled me around.

"Fuck!" I tried to pull away before I realized it was Maka's arms that slipped around me, his scent enveloping me, and I slowly relaxed.

"Sorry," Maka said sheepishly.

"You scared the shit out of me," I admonished, slapping his arm. I'm sure he could feel my heart thundering in my chest.

"I said I was sorry. I just wanted to take a moment, with us being away from everyone else, to tell you how much this means to me. You didn't have to do all of this."

"I kind of did," I said, running my hands up and down the strong planes of his pecs through his shirt.

"Let me show you my gratitude." Maka captured my lips in a sweet kiss. He tried to deepen it, but I pulled back.

"Not that I don't appreciate the gesture," I started, and Maka chuckled, low and deep in his chest. "What?"

"I can feel just how much you appreciate it."

Realizing my erection was grinding against his thigh, I blushed.

"What I'm saying is you couldn't find a better place to show your appreciation than in front of the restroom?"

"Trust me, this is just a prelude to gratitude. The full thing I can't show you in public."

A shiver of excitement went straight to my cock.

"Then why are we still here, exactly?"

"I've been asking myself that question since about four minutes after we got here."

WE MADE EXCUSES quickly after that and beat an exit fifteen minutes later. We didn't talk on the ride home, and we didn't need to; we knew where each other's minds were and where our bodies soon would be.

"Your place or mine?" Maka finally asked when I turned the car into my parking spot.

"Your bed is more comfortable," I pointed out.

"Your door is closer."

"Fine. Mine."

We hurried to my door. As I dug my key out of my pocket, Maka ground himself against me, the prominent bulge of his hard-on pulsing. He wanted it bad. Then again, so did I. The damn key just wouldn't work fast enough.

I finally got the door open and all but fell through it as Maka ushered me in, kicking it closed with one foot while his hands were already hard at work undoing his belt.

I shucked my shirt over my head, tossing it aimlessly aside and fell to my knees. I impatiently pushed Maka's hands aside and undid the button and zipper of his pants before yanking them down. His cock had already pushed its way through the fly of his boxers and pointed toward me.

I was in too much of a sexual state to take the time to admire it or go slow; I gripped his cock by the base and took it into my mouth. I stopped when I'd overreached and taken too much too fast, pulling back before I could gag. I took a deep breath and went back at it, a little slower this time, until I had his full length in my mouth. I'd never been much good at deepthroating, and I'd been okay with that. Something about Maka made me want to be good at it. It was also just a lot of fun practicing on Maka.

Maka looked down at me, watching as I sucked him, eyes hooded with lust. "Goddamn, baby, you do that so good."

I tried to smile up at him around his thick cock, though I doubted he could tell considering how stretched my lips already were.

Maka began thrusting his hips, his cock sliding over my tongue and between my lips. My hands dropped down to free my cock from the confines of my clothes, aching for skin-to-skin contact. It was all I could do not to furiously beat myself off right there.

I don't know how long I spent sucking Maka's cock, but my jaw had begun to ache. Maka had a talent for knowing when that was. He pulled his cock slowly out of my mouth. It came free with a lewd, wet popping noise.

"I think we need a shower," he said, his voice at least an octave lower than it usually was.

"But that takes so much time," I protested. I was thinking entirely with my cock now, and it did not want to be denied instant gratification.

"Shower," Maka repeated, reaching down and pulling me to my feet easily. "Now."

I complied, then, my cock jolting a bit at the commanding tone in Maka's voice. We both left a trail of clothing behind us until we entered the bathroom, naked. As I got towels from the linen closet, Maka's hands were all over me, his cock, slick with my spit and pre-come, gliding between my asscheeks.

"Hurry up." His breath tickled my ear. His fingers had come around my chest and found my nipples, tweaking and tugging them gently.

"I could go faster if you weren't doing that."

He reluctantly removed his hands and stepped back from me. I was disappointed, but the sooner I got this crap out of the way, the sooner in the shower together. I dropped the towels haphazardly on the still-sparkling tile floor and hurried into the shower, turning the spray to pulsate and near-scalding where I knew Maka liked it.

Maka grabbed me by the waist and pressed my body against the cold wall, his lips claiming mine in a fierce kiss, our tongues dancing together. Never breaking contact, Maka reached for the body soap with one hand, using its easy push cap to fill his hand, which he immediately applied to my body. He didn't soap up my chest or back, though; his hand went right to my cock.

The slippery body wash sent wave after wave of sensation through my hypersensitive cock. I shuddered, my toes curling.

Maka finally broke the kiss, smiling almost predatorily. "Feel good?" I nodded, but that wasn't enough for him. "Does it feel good, Gabe?"

"Yes," I managed, voice sounding clunky and unfamiliar to my own ears.

"What about this?" He slid his soap-slicked hand lower, beneath my balls until his fingers were teasing my puckered hole.

"God, yes." I didn't bother to hold back a moan as Maka slipped his middle finger inside, the thick digit opening me—though nowhere near as much as his dick would. I wrapped my arms around Maka's neck, pulling him in for a kiss as he continued to probe his finger deeper inside me.

His index finger soon joined his middle finger, slowly moving in and out of me to give me a chance to adjust to the size. I wasn't really in much of a mood for slow and steady at the moment, though. His cock inside me was all I could think about as the hot water sprayed down on us, steam billowing into the enclosed space, fogging up the glass.

Maka broke the kiss. "Turn around."

He helped me turn and press my front against the tile wall, face turned away from the spray of the shower, back arched out toward him. I heard the pump of the shower gel and the sound of him slicking his cock.

About a week after we got together, Maka and I went to the local health clinic and got a full battery of STD tests. When we both came back clean for everything we'd begun having sex without a condom. It was something I'd never done before, even with Trevor. It required a deep level of trust—and I had that trust with Maka. Since then, sex had taken on a much deeper and more intense meaning for both of us. At least I hoped he felt that way too.

I felt Maka line himself up against my hole and had to fight to stop myself from tensing up. The initial pain of entry was still there even now, but it would pass quickly. I took a deep breath and exhaled as his thick cock entered me. He went slow, and by the time he was fully inside me, the pain had faded to a mild discomfort, and that was quickly forgotten as the blunt head of his cock rubbed against that place deep inside me that turned my legs to jelly.

"You okay?" Maka asked, leaning forward and raining kisses down on my shoulders, neck and jaw.

"Yeah," I said, eyes closed tightly as I let myself get lost in the sensation.

At my assurance, Maka began to thrust, one hand holding my hip, the other slipping between me and the wall to grip my cock, creating a tunnel, so that every time he drove his cock into me it drove my own into the tight ring of his fingers.

The shower was filled with the sound of wet flesh slapping and the grunts we made. It had been several days since either of us had had sex, and it wasn't meant to last. Far too soon, I felt the bubble of orgasm just behind my navel, and then it was on me, my body locking up as I unloaded against the shower wall.

Maka withdrew from me then, jerking himself to his own orgasm, his come striking the shower floor and my ass, to be washed away by the pulsing water. In the aftermath the only thing that kept me from buckling to the floor was Maka's supporting weight.

After I recovered myself, I leaned forward, placing my cheek against Maka's chest. "Goddamn that was good."

Maka made a noise in agreement.

I looked down at the leftover remnants of both our orgasms, slowly being pushed along the shower floor toward the drain.

"Aw," I said wanly. "I just scrubbed that."

Chapter Twelve

THE LOOK OF surprise on Grace's face when she walked in to find me sitting on the desk that used to be Hayley's, Styrofoam cup of coffee extended toward her was great. Everything seemed right with the world now that Maka and I had worked out our problems, and it even motivated me to get out of bed and get to work. It was the first time in a long time that I was the first one there.

"You had sex last night," Grace said, taking the coffee from me with a grateful nod. "Glad you and Maka worked everything out. It *was* with Maka, right?"

"Yes," I said, exasperated she'd even imply otherwise.

"Just making sure. You seem to be in such a better mood now."

"I am. Thank you for noticing."

"It's amazing what sex can do for you."

"It's not the sex," I argued, even though it partly was. "It's knowing that things are fine between Maka and I. I'm ready to throw myself into work without worries about my relationship hanging over my head."

"That's good to hear, because Jin called me this morning," Grace said, going into the back and opening her office door.

"Morning love chats, now?" I teased, following her.

"Nope, not yet—it will happen, that I promise you—but he's coming by around nine-thirty with some more information he says is really important. It sounds like he's cracked the case wide open."

"Well, as long as I didn't have to do it. Contracting out is good. Why don't we do that with all the roles and just take the money?"

"Because then we'd have no money," she said. "For fuck's sake, look at all this paperwork I have. It's going to take forever."

"Is that still paperwork on the Evans job? We did that right after we opened this office, Grace! I told you to stay on top of your paperwork."

"I'll pay you one hundred dollars to do it for me," she said hopefully, making a pouty face.

"Nope. Not a chance." I turned on my heel and walked into my office, pretty sure she'd thrown her middle finger up at me. Once situated at my desk, I called out to her, "Someone should let Biers know Jin's coming, too."

"You're right," she said just as I said, "Not it!"

"Damn it! I really wish you'd go back to being melancholy and depressed."

It was a quiet thirty minutes before Jin showed up. Not far behind him was Biers. I didn't know exactly what Grace had told him, but whatever it was definitely made him happy. He looked like a puppy with his favorite toy being waved in his face.

The moment he was through the door he reached for Jin, holding his shoulders. "Is it true? Did you really find the treasure?"

"Woah, woah," Jin said, clearly caught off guard. He stepped back from Biers's hands. "Let's not get all hasty here, bro. I'm not entirely sure what I found."

"But you found something," Biers pressed.

Jin nodded, grinning. "I did. Whoever wrecked my shit must have thought I wouldn't be able to access the data, but I just used a different device. Never think a tech guy doesn't have access to more equipment. Anyway, I managed to get the files on the Cloud server I'd missed. Most of them were concerning map coordinates."

Biers's eyes widened so much I thought they would explode. "So you *did* find the treasure!"

"I can't say that for certain, but yeah, I think so."

I couldn't believe it. I figured that one of these days Biers would realize it was a pipe dream and wasn't ever going to come true. Now it was starting to look like we had a map? I wasn't a fan of pie in the best of circumstances—I was much more a cake kind of guy—and humble pie was the worst.

Is it terrible of me to hope we find nothing there?

"We have coordinates! We have coordinates!" Biers jumped up and down like a giddy child. Even Grace looked excited.

"We're going to go and find actual buried treasure!"

I looked on, torn between bemusement and embarrassment, as the two of them did a little dance together.

"There's something else, too," Jin added, and the tone of his voice caused Grace and Biers's smiles to falter a bit. "Someone accessed these files today. Probably whoever broke my stuff. They must have gotten in and reset the password using my hacks."

"How do you know that?" I inquired.

"The Cloud server also functions as a sharing site, so it has the number of times downloaded listed—even for files not made public. A download happened today that wasn't me. Since the owner is dead, I can't imagine he did it, either. It had to be the vandals."

Biers's face grew stony. "Which means they might already have the treasure."

"Maybe."

"Damn it!" Biers pulled slightly at his hair—which explained how it was his hair got into the kinky mess I was used to seeing on him.

"Calm down, Mr. Biers," I said, worried he might actually pull his hair out.

"You don't understand! How could you? You've spent a week on this job, but I've spent *years* of my life on it! *Years!* If someone else gets it before I do, then I'll have wasted all of that time, and my friends will be dead for no reason!"

"There's a chance he hasn't found it yet," Grace assured Biers, putting an arm around his shoulder comfortingly. "We should look at this as an opportunity, you know."

I frowned as Grace's face took on a mischievous cast. "I don't like that look, Grace. That's your 'I'm planning something' look, and it never ends well."

"Listen, if it *is* Rice who is behind all this, he'll be wherever the coordinates lead, right? We can catch him in the act!"

"I refer you back to my earlier remark about these things not ending well," I said, unable to fathom how she could possibly think this is a good idea.

"I checked the coordinates. They seem to be on the ocean," Jin added.

"Which means we have time!" Grace exclaimed. "Think about it—it's almost impossible to book a boat or rent one less than a day in advance! We still have a shot at this."

"You're not helping," I told Jin sourly. "Grace, this is an awful idea. We need to call the police and let them handle it from here. People are *dead* remember? And I don't want to join that rank anytime soon."

"We'll be fine." Grace waved away my concerns—very legitimate ones, I thought.

"How about this? Since it's only Rice and me left, and it seems like he's the one responsible for that, why don't I increase your stake to forty percent?"

"That's *so much money*, Gabe! Think of what we could do with it. Advertising, for one thing! Come on, please?"

"No. I'm not going. You can if you want to, but I'm not."

Grace put her hands on her hips. "I'm going to call your bluff on that. I'm in, Gabe. I want to go on a treasure hunt. I want to prove this guy's behind the whole thing."

"And what will you do when you prove that?" I cried.

"We'll call the cops and have them come swooping in, of course," she said haughtily.

I groaned, covering my face with both hands. I swore Grace was going to drive me prematurely gray. "You're not going to change your mind on this, are you?"

"Not a chance in hell."

"Damn it. I can't let you go do something this stupid alone. So I guess I'm going to do it with you."

"Great!"

"I'm in too," Jin said, sounding almost as eager as Grace and Biers.

Am I the only sane person I know?

An idea struck me, then, a subtle way to get revenge. "On one condition," I added, raising a finger. "I get to pick the next secretary."

Grace shrugged it off. "That's all? Sure, go ahead."

I gave her an evil look, and her confident smile began to fade as she realized she might have made a mistake.

"Jin, what was your neighbor's name, the lovely woman with the cane?"

"Mrs. Neidermeyer?"

"That's the one. I seem to recall she was at a job fair Saturday."

I wiggled my eyebrows at Grace. Well, my version, since I couldn't get them to do it properly. It consisted mostly of me raising and lowering them rapidly. "Why don't you give her our number and see if she's interested in a secretarial position."

Grace cursed under her breath.

"I'm going to go right now and see if I can charter a boat!" Biers bounded for the door, barely looking over his shoulder as he added, "I'll be in contact shortly!"

I SPENT THE morning trying to convince Grace how dangerous this whole situation was in hopes that she'd be reasonable. We'd provided Biers with the information he needed to find his treasure, so we'd fulfilled our end of the bargain.

Grace wasn't having it, though. She was caught up in the romanticism of it all—buried treasure, World War II secrets, a race to get it before the bad guys. I could practically see her imagining herself as a female Indiana Jones or Nathan Drake. The problem with that was Grace tended to be reckless at the best of times, and imagining herself a roguish hero would just up the danger.

I thought I had a chance to change her mind when Mrs. Niedermeyer came to the office—unannounced—to interview for the position of secretary. She was wearing all name brand things, from the looks of it. Her blouse was far too low-cut for a woman of her age, her jeans hanging just a bit low on her hips. I couldn't help but notice she didn't have the cane.

I thought Grace would have a nervous breakdown with Mrs. Niedermeyer there. Everything about the old lady—from her refusal to give up her social security number to us, fearing it to be a scam to steal her identity, to her firm insistence she'd set her own schedule and it would have to work around her Mahjong tournaments—seemed to drive Grace crazy. By the end of the fifteen-minute interview, where she asked *us* questions instead of the other way around, Grace's right eye had a nervous twitch and she was grinding her teeth so hard I thought I'd hear them crack.

"You're hired," I said to Mrs. Niedermeyer, based solely on how much fun I anticipated having watching Grace go slowly crazy from her presence. "You can start tomorrow."

"I'll start the day after tomorrow," Mrs. Niedermeyer countered. "Tomorrow there's an all-day *Diagnosis Murder* marathon I want to catch."

"I think she's going to be a good fit," I told Grace, smiling serenely.

"I hate you so much," she growled, stomping back to pout in her office.

Just before four, Biers called Grace to let her know he'd chartered a boat to take us to the coordinates the next morning. He gave us an address at a pier to meet him at, insisting we be there by a quarter past nine, because the boat would leave promptly at ten.

"On that note I'm going home," I informed Grace. "By the way, tonight I figured I would make stir-fry and watch *The Wiz*, if you wanted to join me."

"No Maka tonight?"

"He's got something or other that will keep him late. He'll be over around midnight. Until then, feel free to come by."

"Okay, one question: did you hire Neidermeyer just to annoy me?"

"Grace," I said, feigning shock. "I'm hurt that you would even ask that question."

"So that's a yes."

"Yup."

"I hate you."

"See you at seven!"

"I won't be there! Wait, stir-fry? Yes, I will."

The evening passed quietly with stir-fry and *The Wiz*, one of my all-time favorite movies. Grace was good company, having gotten over the hiring of Mrs. Neidermeyer. We chatted about random things—mostly her borderline obsession with Jin and how we could turn her dream into a reality. I resisted the urge to point out that she sounded just this side of stalker-ish, feeling like she needed the support more than she needed the teasing. Besides, if the sense I'd gotten was right, Jin more than returned her interest.

Not long after Grace left, Maka came in, looking absolutely worn out.

"Long day?" I asked as I hurried to put the leftover stir-fry into the microwave for him.

"Dead body washed up on the beach," he said, dropping down onto the couch and throwing his head back, eyes closed and face turned toward the ceiling. "Straightforward, though; looks like someone was jogging near the beach and got mugged. Whoever did it didn't bother hiding a lot of evidence, thinking the ocean would destroy most of it."

The microwave beeped, and I grabbed a fork and joined him in the living room, placing the plate on the coffee table. "But you found something?"

"The vic got a few good swipes in at her attacker, apparently. We found some foreign DNA under her fingernails. We're expecting to have it matched to someone soon. Assuming the guy is in the system, which I think he would be. Probably petty theft and similar mugging."

Maka sat up, having gathered something of a second wind, looking at the stir-fry with great interest. "Is this take-out stir-fry or homemade?"

"It's homemade," I said proudly. Maka gave it a second appraisal, face turning wary. "Eat it."

Maka made a show of his first bite, acting like he was eating something foreign or unpleasant. He could be an ass when he wanted to be.

"It's delicious," he said after torturing me.

"You enjoy being an asshole, don't you?"

He grinned. "On occasion."

We sat there in companionable silence while he ate. An old *Andy Griffith Show* episode was on television, though neither of us paid it much attention. I tried my best to stay focused on Maka's presence, but I found it harder and harder to keep my mind from thoughts of the next day. With each passing minute, my anxiety grew worse and worse, approaching the overwhelming point. I didn't let Maka see, though. I flashed him a smile every time he looked at me.

Maka was tired, so we opted for bed not long after he finished eating. Maka fell asleep quickly, but I couldn't so easily escape my own thoughts. It was stupid of us to go traipsing after someone we suspected of murder. Rice had already proven himself more than willing to kill for this treasure—a dozen times over, if the reports of deaths were to be believed. Why put ourselves at risk like that?

I'd said as much to Grace over stir-fry, and all she said was, "You did it looking for Carrie's killer." She was right, of course, but the circumstances were entirely different, and she knew that. I would do anything for her, but I couldn't say the same for Edwin Biers.

But at that moment, I didn't need to be rehashing earlier conversations or thinking about Biers or Rice or anything. I needed to be sleeping.

I tried changing my position. I tried counting sheep—I made it to forty-three before I felt too ridiculous to continue. I even tried controlled breathing, but nothing worked. I looked despondently at the clock on my nightstand. 2:02 am, and I was still awake. I felt like something was going to come bursting out of me, so at last I rolled over to face Maka and shook him awake.

"What is it? What's wrong?" Maka asked blearily, sitting up in bed, seemingly looking around for signs of danger.

"Nothing's wrong, exactly," I said, suddenly regretting waking him up.

Maka glowered at the clock. "It's two in the morning."

"I know. I can't sleep."

"So that means I don't get to either? That doesn't sound fair."

I fidgeted guiltily, and Maka slipped his arm around me, pulling me to rest against his chest.

"I just needed to talk to someone," I admired, getting comfortable. "You just happen to be available."

He snorted. "Thanks."

"I feel like I'm going nuts, okay?"

"What is it?" Maka asked, his hand stroking up and down my bare forearm soothingly.

I filled him in on everything that had transpired with Biers—the deaths we'd discovered, Rice's suspected involvement.

"Why didn't you report any of this?" Maka scolded gently when I was done.

"And say what? 'I think these random deaths happening all over the country are connected to this one guy'? The police have already had their say in these deaths. As far as they are concerned, these are all accidental."

"This is a terrible idea," Maka said flatly. "You can't seriously be going to those coordinates, considering you think a murderer will be there too."

"It's not like I want to! But Grace is in. I tried to talk her out of it, but I wasn't successful. And there's no way I'm letting her go and do something like this on her own."

"She'll have Biers and that tech guy with her."

I quirked an eyebrow. "You think that's comforting? She needs someone who isn't blinded by the possibility of this treasure."

Maka was quiet for a moment, and then he said, "Have you realized that all of the trouble you've gotten into has been her fault?"

"Trust me, it's crossed my mind."

"You know what, I'm going with you tomorrow."

I blinked. "What?"

"You heard me."

I wanted so much to accept his offer, wanted to tell him to please come and talk some sense into these people, but I knew that, no matter how good of an idea I thought it was, it simply couldn't happen.

"Unfortunately, as much as I want you to, you can't. We have a confidentiality clause in our contract. If Biers finds out I've told you anything, he can get out of paying us for our services. We need the money for this job."

"So you expect me to let you go after this treasure with a maniac waiting for you?"

"Yes, but this could be a good thing, right?" I sat up and faced him full on. "We could catch a murderer hoping to sell stolen goods on the Black Market. I'm also not entirely convinced Biers plans on returning the goods to the Japanese government. If I go to the island, you'll have a way of catching Rice in the act while also ensuring the stolen goods in the tontine go back to Japan where they belong."

"Won't that look suspicious? Wouldn't Biers say you violated the confidentiality clause?"

"I might have an idea about that, so leave it to me. The contract says we help him find the tontine, not that we make sure it remains in his hands. I think this might work."

Maka didn't look too pleased, but he nodded. "Okay, fine. But if we're going to do it, we're going to do it my way—got it?"

"I like when you take charge," I said with a wink. "Tell me what you had in mind."

MORNING CAME FAR too quickly for my taste. I felt like I'd barely closed my eyes and now here I was waking up. By the time Maka and I finished all the arrangements necessary to do this his way, Grace and Jin arrived in Grace's Jeep to take us to the boat.

Honolulu Harbor was massive, filled with tourists, workers, and people just out to have a good time. The harbor played host not only to professional boats belonging to fishermen or people who conducted island tours, but also privately owned boats. The collection ranged from expensive yachts to modest boats and sailboats to motorboats meant for water sports. They were of varying sizes and conditions. Some looked pretty beat-up, pieced together by spare or salvaged parts, while others looked as if they were top of the line and probably cost a small fortune.

I didn't like the idea of being on a boat in the middle of the ocean, so I prayed the boat Biers chartered wasn't one of the rusty buckets.

Jin, Grace, and I looked around the front of the harbor, searching for any sign of Biers.

"Where is he?" Grace muttered, checking her watch. "It's ten till ten. I figured he'd be here by now."

"I figured he was here all night," I muttered. It did seem odd to me that he'd not be here when he'd been so damn excited about this whole thing in the first place. I started to get the feeling something was wrong.

"Over here! Guys, over here!"

I looked up and saw Biers waving his arms in the air, signaling us toward one of the nearby row of berths. I wasn't quite relieved when I saw him, but I was glad nothing was wrong. The last thing we needed was for Biers to turn up dead, too.

"I thought you weren't going to make it," Biers admitted, turning on his heel and hurrying along the quay.

"We were here on time." Grace sounded just the slightest bit testy. "You just didn't tell us where to come to meet you."

"Well, you're here now, and that's what matters."

Grace caught my look and rolled her eyes.

The more boats we passed, the more my confidence fell. At first they were all nice boats, probably the sort that someone middle class could afford with a helpful bank loan. The farther along we went, though, the worse they became. I was pretty sure if we reached the end of the pier, we'd be looking at a rubber inner tube with plastic paddles.

Maybe it wasn't too late to back out of all of this.

"Here she is," Biers said finally, coming to a stop in front of a moderately-sized boat. It didn't look cutting edge or top of the line, but nor did it look like an aluminium can bobbing in the water. It was the right size for five or six people to board comfortably.

"I'm not so sure about this," Grace muttered to me, looking at the boat. The captain, a swarthy man who looked to be of some sort of Eastern European descent, stood on the side and greeted us with a cool wave. His face was impassive, his eyes hard as stone.

"Don't worry," I told her, taking her hand and squeezing it. "You know how protective Maka is. If something goes wrong and we don't turn up, he'll come looking for us."

"How's he going to find us in the middle of the ocean?" Grace asked.

"Trace our phones, probably," Jin answered for me.

I nodded. "Exactly. Maka told me he'd come looking for us if we were back before sunset. So, if something goes wrong, we know Maka's out there ready to come and save the day."

I didn't realize Biers had overheard until he spoke. "Who's Maka?"

"Gabe's boyfriend," Grace answered. "He's a cop. A homicide detective, actually."

"Well, good to know someone's out there waiting for us if Daniel pulls something. Now come on, let's get onboard and get after that treasure."

"Before we do, I want to ask you a question." I could see Biers's impatience, but he nodded his go-ahead. "After everything that's happened—the deaths of your cohorts, the betrayal by Rice, is this worth it?"

"Yes." Biers didn't even hesitate when he gave his answer. "It's very much worth it. If we find this, we'll go down in history—and we can make sure that Rice pays and Alvin and Tolly and the others all get the recognition they deserve. Now, what are we waiting for? Let's go!"

Biers hopped aboard, and Grace followed. The boat's captain, who Biers never introduced us to, offered her his hand to help her up. I went behind Jin, a jolt of something I couldn't name going through me as I set my feet on the boat's deck, as if I'd crossed some sort of invisible line between the dock and the boat. In a way I had, and there was no turning back.

Chapter Thirteen

"DO WE KNOW how long this ride will take?" I asked Biers as the captain slowly navigated the boat free of its berth, slowly turning us toward a heading out to sea.

"When I gave the captain the coordinates yesterday, he told me about thirty, thirty-five minutes."

Two sides of the boat were lined with long benches with a single uncomfortable cushion. The captain steered the boat from the front, and between them was an expanse that rose into the air, shading a set of stairs that led down to a cabin belowdecks.

I noticed we all opted to stay topside.

Even sitting on the uncomfortable bench, it was easy to lose track of the tension of the day, with the boat gliding over the waves, the occasional spray spouting over the sides, the sun glistening on the water and a cool ocean breeze, heavy with the scent of salt, caressing my face. I could almost pretend it was pleasure and not business that brought me out there.

But then I got a glimpse of my traveling companions and the illusion came to a shattering end. I doubted anyone would choose Edwin Biers as a partner for a casual outing. I didn't even want to choose him for a work outing.

"How are you not enjoying this?" Grace asked me, stretching her arms out to either side on the rails of the boat, sunglasses on her face, looking like someone out for a day of tanning and not going to work.

"This isn't something we're *supposed* to be enjoying," I reminded her, trying not to be annoyed.

"We're on a boat in the middle of the ocean on a gorgeous day, off to find millions of dollars' worth of treasure! What's not exciting about that?"

"The fact that there's probably someone there with a gun waiting to kill us?" I offered. I couldn't believe how thoroughly wrapped up in the romantic treasure hunting idea Grace had become. "Or the fact that this might also be a colossal waste of time? Maybe these coordinates are Alvin Liu's favorite fishing spot."

Grace shook her head condescendingly, like I just didn't understand something and she felt it was too simple to bother explaining. "Always so negative, Gabe. What are the chances of something going wrong today?"

I pinched the bridge of my nose, wishing she hadn't said that. "With us involved? Pretty damn high."

"Dude, that captain guy is one cold bro," Jin said, coming from the front of the boat and dropping down onto the bench next to Grace, who quickly sat up to make room for him. "Hasn't said one word."

"Speaking of the captain," said Grace thoughtfully, "does anyone else get a strange sense of deja vu when they see him?"

I craned my neck to try to get a glimpse of the captain, but the boat all but blocked my view. I caught a glimpse of a shoulder, but nothing else. It didn't trigger anything for me, so I just shook my head. I noticed Jin did the same.

"I swear I've seen him before," Grace insisted, tapping her index finger against her lip as if it would help her conjure the memory.

"There are only so many people on this island," Biers said from the other bench where he'd been staring out at the ocean, seemingly lost in thought. "Maybe you *have* seen him somewhere out and about."

"I doubt we run in the same circles," Grace mused. "But who knows—you're probably right. Still, something about him seems...I don't know, strange to me."

Biers waved a hand, dismissing her concerns. "I'm sure you're just nervous."

Having had enough of the conversation, I rose and made my way belowdecks. The cabin there resembled an RV: a small space at the back for a bed, a kitchenette with a small mini fridge, a single hot plate and a tiny microwave, and a bathroom that looked to be the width of a refrigerator box.

The bathroom was just as cramped on the inside as it appeared from outside, and I felt claustrophobic while using it. The constant back-and-forth rolling didn't help, either.

Before going back up again, I examined the cabin interior, curious to see if there was any indication of what the boat's owner was like.

Everything was very spartan, with no personal items. Oddly enough, it looked like there had once been picture frames hung on the wall near the bed. The wall was slightly discolored in a few picture-frame-shaped patches, the result of the spots being concealed from the harsh light of the cabin bulb and the sunlight that came in through the porthole near where the walls met the ceiling to either side.

"Maybe a bad breakup," I murmured, trying to think of a reason the pictures might have been taken down. There were a few reasons, but a relationship ending badly might explain the cold distance he affected.

Or he could just be a cold guy; who did I think I was making deductions about the lives and personality of people I'd barely just met?

"You okay down there?" Grace called from the top of the stairs. "You're not seasick, are you?"

"I'm fine," I answered, flushing guiltily. At least no one knew what I was doing down there. I hurried up and into the warm Hawaiian sun. "Never used the bathroom on a boat before."

Grace eyed me suspiciously. "You didn't pee on the seat, did you?"

"I'm not a toddler, Grace!"

"Neither was Trevor."

I paused, thinking about the state my ex frequently left the bathroom in. "Good point. But no, I didn't."

"Would you honestly tell me if you did?"

THE MOTION OF the boat and my tiredness from the night before actually lulled me into a sort of stupor. I didn't quite sleep—if I did, I didn't remember it, at least—but I did zone out for a while, only to be brought back to the present by a loud whoop from the front of the boat.

I got up quickly, stumbling a little bit with the unexpected rolling of the waves. I hurried to the front of the boat, the bow or whatever it was called, half expecting to see pirates looming in the distance, their cannons focused on us, ready to blow us out of the water. What I saw was Jin standing near the captain, nearly jumping up and down with excitement. Grace was leaning *over* the rail at the front of the ship, peering ahead at something.

It took my eyes moment to figure out what it was. It was an island, all right. It had a rocky shore and a dense growth of trees beyond that. It was hard to tell how big it was, but it couldn't have been very large or it would appear on maps. The coast I could see stretched about the length of a football field before curving, so hopefully that's about the size of what we'd be dealing with.

"Goddamn it." Grace straightened suddenly, and I saw why around her. There was a boat at the island already. It looked empty, from what I could tell, and in much worse shape than the one we rode. I was surprised the thing was sea-worthy. Though, if we'd been going farther out, it probably wouldn't have been.

"This proves it," Biers said, coming up next to me. He sounded sad.

I shook my head, the knot returning to my stomach. I thought I'd gotten rid of it after fixing things with Maka, but it was back with a vengeance now, along with an overall sense of foreboding.

"This doesn't prove Rice is behind it. Just that *someone* took the information and used it."

"Which means they might have already found the treasure," Jin said. "What if they have weapons?"

"We'll be fine," Biers said with far more confidence than I felt the situation deserved. "We'll sneak through the forest, stay hidden until they find the treasure or we know they've got it, and then we can call in Gabe's cop boyfriend."

I looked at Biers with a newfound respect. "That was…surprisingly reasonable of you, Mr. Biers."

Biers frowned. "You say that like it's a surprise."

"Let's just say I haven't found a lot of your decisions to fall into the category of what *I* might call reasonable. This one, this one is good."

"I don't want any more death," Biers said, voice heavy with emotion. I reminded myself this was a man who'd devoted his life to something only to very likely be betrayed by someone he'd trusted, and lost people he valued in the process. He was undoubtedly hurt by Rice's betrayal and felt grief over the deaths—and maybe more than just a little self-blame. "I won't endanger any of you. We handle this as safely as we possibly can."

The man steering the boat killed the engines once we reached a certain point, letting the boat's momentum lead us close to shore.

"He'll stay with the boat," Biers informed us. "That way we can get out of here quickly if we need to. If something goes wrong, we should all make for the boat. Let's get going. Be careful and stay in sight of each other."

"Stay as close to Jin and me as you can," I ordered Grace as we hopped out of the boat into knee-deep salt water.

Grace gave me a little sneer. "What? You think I'm going to go wandering off in the woods on a tiny island full of dangerous people?"

"You've been known to do strange things."

Grace gave a small chuckle, shaking her head. The chuckle died when she really caught the look on my face and realized I was dead serious. She sloshed through the water to me before placing her hands on my shoulders and looking me right in the eye.

"Gabe, I promise I'm not going to do something stupid."

I nodded my satisfaction, and she and I followed behind Biers and Jin, who were already wading to shore. It was hard going, because we were trudging over uneven ground and sharp rocks that I felt pressing against my feet through the soles of my shoes. It felt like I was walking on a floor strewn with Lego. It was a relief to finally reach the tree line and some ground that wasn't trying to slice my feet open. I had the insane urge to look at the soles of my shoes, but I didn't want to see the damage inflicted on them. It was better not to know, sometimes.

Right away I noticed a path of sorts, with branches pushed aside, undergrowth trampled on.

"Should we follow it?" Biers asked, the question directed more at me than anyone else. Why was I, the one more adamantly against this in the first place, suddenly being asked to make decisions about it? Maybe, though, that was for the best.

"No. We don't know who's on it. It's safer to approach slowly from off-path, somewhere we can hide and watch. Everybody cool with that?" I looked at Biers, Jin, and Grace. The first two nodded their agreement. Grace just looked downcast. "What's wrong, Grace?" *Maybe she's going to say let's just turn around and get back on the boat. Maybe she's come to her senses.*

"I should have worn long sleeves. My arms are going to be so itchy after this."

I scowled. "Let's just go already."

We formed a sort of straight line, Biers at the front, me at the back, and Grace in front of me and behind Jin. We stopped every dozen steps or so for Biers to choose a path. He kept us on the one that provided the least resistance while still being fairly well concealed from the makeshift path to our left. It was slow going, but being safe was much better than being stupid in my book. Then again, we were being stupid doing this at all.

Every time I heard a noise I jumped—whether it was a twig snapping because of a misplaced foot or the sound of a particularly loud ocean swell against the rocks or my own breathing catching my attention. This couldn't be good for our health. Stress was bad for the body, right? Well, it didn't get much more stressful.

"Shit," Biers whispered ahead of me, and I nearly toppled the whole line like dominoes when I didn't realize we'd stopped. I had to grab Grace around the waist to keep her from losing her balance.

"What's wrong?" Jin asked Biers, only to get shushed. I looked around Grace to see Biers point toward the trail. I moved my body until I had a good view through the trees and caught sight of a man dressed in dark clothes there on the path, not more than ten feet away from us.

I held my breath, wishing I could will my heart to stop beating. It drummed so loudly in my ears I couldn't imagine how anyone else didn't hear it. The moment seemed to be suspended in time. Would the man hear or see us? If he did, it would mean the end of the entire ordeal; we would have no choice but to beat a retreat to the boat, tails between our legs, and go home. If we didn't get shot in the process.

Miraculously, the man started away, farther inland. He hadn't noticed us. How was that even possible?

The four of us traded relieved looks. Biers gestured over his shoulder with his thumb, probably signaling that we should put a little more distance between ourselves and the path these men were using. He would get no argument from me there.

Biers took a step back and that terrible, rotten luck Grace and I shared kicked in. He stepped right onto a dried, old twig. It snapped loudly, and dread filled Grace and Jin's faces, a look I knew was mirrored on my own.

"Who's out there?" a gruff voice called.

"Go," Biers hissed, pushing Jin's shoulder roughly. "Go, go! Back to the boat!"

"Hey!"

We were spotted.

There was no more time to think; I just lurched forward, running through the trees and retracing our steps. For a moment, it felt like I'd never left the rainforest. *If I get out of this alive, I'm never going to another forest in my life. Fuck nature, it's overrated.*

The sudden appearance of a black-clad man ahead forced a detour, and I darted off to the left, away from the trail. How had someone gotten around behind us? Had they known we were there all along?

"Grace, you okay?" I called, panting. I risked a quick glance over my shoulder and saw Grace was no longer behind me. *Fuck. Fuck, fuck, fuck.* Where had she gone? Panic surged in me, hot and bitter, bile burning the back of my throat.

Hold it together, Gabe. She probably saw the same guy and went the other way. She's making for the boat. We're all making for the boat.

The rocky beach I'd despised earlier became the most beautiful sight in the world as I broke out of the trees. I could no longer run or else risk breaking my leg or twisting my ankle on the uneven rocks, but the men chasing us wouldn't be able to either. And the boat was just ahead of me.

No one is there yet, I realized. The others were still in the trees. Had they been caught? Were they dead? Was *Grace* dead?

It was no time to panic, though. I needed to keep a steady head about me to handle this. *Right. Get on the boat, call Maka, and get help. That's the best I can do for them right now.*

I crossed the rocky beach, keeping my head ducked low. Every now and then, I looked over my shoulders but found no sign of someone following me, which I found to be very odd. There had been someone right behind me, and it had to have been obvious where I was headed.

The owner of the boat was standing in the water near the boat as I approached, and I was relieved. In some part of my mind, I'd been worried the boat had been somehow taken, cutting off any hope of getting back to Honolulu safely.

"They spotted us," I called to the man, wading out toward him. "The others are probably on the way. You should get the boat ready to go."

I made my way past him, reaching for the railing to pull myself up into the boat. Before I could lever myself up, though, the boat owner's hand clamped down on my shoulder, hard. I didn't get to ask him what he was doing as I found myself jerked down from the boat, nearly falling into the water. He used his grip on my shoulder to turn me around, his broad hand reaching out and striking me across the face, an open-palmed slap that left me dazed enough for him to hoist me up over his shoulders, my head and arms hanging over one, my legs over the other, held in such a way that I could offer no resistance.

Didn't stop me from trying, though. I felt like a fish, flopping around on his shoulders. If I could just work my ankles or wrists free of the vice grip I could maybe have a better shot of getting away from him. Or at least get to my phone.

The man marched with me on his shoulders like I was no heavier to him than a backpack and the beach was gentle sand and not rock.

"How did Rice get to you?" I demanded. "He come to see you after Biers, giving a deal if you work for him instead of us? How much money did he offer?"

I knew the man wasn't going to answer my questions, but talking was the only thing allowing me to keep a grip on my control. Otherwise I'd be screaming. Chances were I still might start.

Once we entered the trees I had to tuck my head into my arms as well as I could to protect my face from the low-hanging leaves and branches. Boat Guy didn't seem to care if my face got scratched—didn't seem to care how much pain the rough jostling was causing my side, either.

"Here's one," he said at last, and I looked up.

He'd taken me to what looked to be a dig site for the tontine. It was a wide clearing, large enough for seven or eight people to camp comfortably. Harold Graham and his fellow soldiers had taken the time to install their own fire pit that was still there. Several holes had been begun, some a little further along than others. There were only two others there then, both the same men who'd been in the Coffee Barn. The others must still be out chasing down the others. That was good; it meant there was still a chance.

Or so I thought until I heard one of them say, "Just drop him next to that one."

They'd caught one of us. Goddamn it, I knew this was a bad idea. I winced hard when Boat Guy dropped me hard on the ground. I scrambled away from him until my back was pressed against a tree.

"Mr. Maxfield?"

The voice caught me off guard, and I turned to see Daniel Rice against the same tree. He looked genuinely surprised to see me. It took a second for my mind to register that there were ropes tied around his wrists and ankles.

My voice returned, flooded by anger. "Daniel Rice. What happened? Your goon squad get greedy and turn against you, too?

"My goon—?"

"You deserve it," I went on, not giving him a chance to voice his phony defenses. "After everything you've done."

"Everything I've done? I don't know what you're talking about, Mr. Maxfield!"

I shook my head in pity. "The lies won't work, Rice. We know about the deaths, all of it, and we know about Jin Hamada's computers. I mean, you're here, and that's proof enough."

"Proof of what? These men kidnapped me in the middle of the night and dragged me here, tied up, and you think I'm behind it?"

"You're not going to trick me," I insisted. "The person responsible had to know about the hunt, had to be in on intimate knowledge regarding the tontine, our movements. If not you, then who?"

"Looks like we've got another one," I heard Boat Guy say, cutting off my tirade. I glanced up as two men came along, pulling a struggling Jin behind them. His nose was bloody and it looked like his eye was slowly swelling shut, so they'd clearly had to use force to get control of him.

But where was Grace?

The answer to that question came seconds later when Grace also emerged from the trees into the clearing. She was walking of her own accord, it seemed, though she was stiff and her expression fearful. Biers came behind her, looking surprisingly calm. I didn't fully understand what was going on until he shoved Grace and Jin over to where Rice and I sat and I caught sight of the gun in Biers's hand.

Chapter Fourteen

"WHAT...WHAT'S GOING on?" I demanded, struggling to wrap my mind around everything I was seeing. Grace drew up close to me, Jin on her other side. I could feel Grace's body trembling from fear.

"What ever do you mean, Mr. Maxfield?" Biers asked me, voice overflowing with condescension. "This is exactly what we agreed to, right? We're finally going to unearth the damn tontine."

I took Grace's hand and gave it a comforting squeeze. "So all of this, it was a setup? The men following you, the high-speed chase, the paranoia—all of it was so we'd never suspect you and turn our attention to Rice while you continued doing whatever you were doing behind our backs? I said from the beginning there was something about you I didn't like. Now I know what it is: you're a sonofabitch."

"You're only half right, I'm afraid. These men were partially a smokescreen to keep suspicion off me, that much is true, but I didn't set out to frame Daniel. *You're* the one who directed everyone's attention toward him, and once you'd done that, I realized how useful it could be, so I decided to use it."

I chanced a glance at Rice, who had turned a hurt look on me. "Sorry." When the reproachful look didn't pass, I added, "Hey, he's the one who lied to all of us. Be mad at him, not me."

"Mr. Maxfield is right." Rice turned to Biers. "For the last *three years*, you've been lying to me—you lied to all of us. Alvin, Tolly, KitKat, all of us. And then you killed them and made it look like accidents."

"What? Of course I didn't." Biers gestured to the men standing around him. As we'd been talking, several had returned, until there was a total of seven of them. "How could I kill people all over the country? These guys did it for me. About the lies, though, not really. My interest in the tontine was obviously real. I just lied about why and how it came about. I've been searching for the tontine for nearly five years."

"You didn't buy the estate property that told you about it until..." Rice trailed off, his confusion evident on his face. "It didn't come from an estate sale, did it?"

Biers smiled coldly, pointing at Rice. "*Ding-ding-ding.* No, the information about the tontine came from my grandfather."

"So your grandfather was one of the original tontine members?" Grace surmised.

"Beauty and brains, I like that." Biers gave Grace an almost lecherous look of approval. "Yes, he was. I never paid much attention to his old war stories—the old bastard had dementia, and it seemed like nonsense most of the time. Then, in one of his rare moments of clarity, he told me about the tontine, how he was almost the last, if he could just outlive Graham. I got him to explain everything to me, but he couldn't remember where they hid it, or what was in it, just that it was worth a lot of money and almost his. That was his last lucid moment, and he died not long after."

"How did Rice and the others get involved?" I asked, thinking that any moment he spent talking was more time we could hope for help to come. It was a ridiculous hope, of course; Maka didn't have a psychic sense that would tell him I was in danger. The plan was for me to somehow get a signal to him, something he could use to come sweeping in, or else wait until sundown.

I was starting to regret not bringing him with us.

"Originally I intended to search myself. I didn't think I needed any help. That just meant more people involved, people I would have to share my information with, and that would be risky. I lurked on the outskirts of the message boards and groups you all used, hoping one of you would inadvertently give me something useful. I spent nearly two years doing that. When it didn't work, I started reaching out. When I had your trust, Daniel, I shared some modified information about the tontine. The journal was fake—I needed a reasonable way to say I understood what was going on without explaining that the information came from one of the last surviving members."

"Where do Grace and I come in?" I inquired. "I don't get why you bothered to seek us out at all."

"Once we got here, I still didn't have any idea where the treasure was, and there was still some groundwork to be done. I thought it would be simple to use you after I saw your faces in the newspaper."

"Remember when you said there's no such thing as bad press?" I asked Grace.

"How the hell was I supposed to know a crazy man would target us because of it?"

Biers let out a sigh. "I'm not crazy. I just want to be a very rich man. With your help, I will be. So thank you. Oh, before I forget. Take your phones out, all of you. Now."

Grace and Jin looked like they wanted to resist, but I shook my head. It was not worth fighting at this point, not worth pissing off a guy with a gun. I took my phone out and tossed it over toward Biers, Grace and Jin following suit. Biers pointed to the phones and two of his men hefted shovels and smashed them to bits.

"That phone cost me damn near a thousand bucks!" Jin complained. "You guys keep destroying my tech. Not cool."

"Oh, I wouldn't worry about that," said Biers, stomping on the shattered remains of our phones. "You're not going to have much need for expensive tech soon."

"So you're going to kill us." Grace's words weren't a question, and they didn't sound scared. "What, you couldn't have come up with a more original plan?"

"I had a science teacher who used to always tell me the key to anything is the KISS method: keep it simple, stupid. I'm keeping it simple. Before I kill you, though, you're going to help me dig up the tontine. Get up. Not you, Daniel; you're the guest of honor, so stay seated."

Grace, Jin, and I stood, taking the proffered shovels. The men shoved us toward the deepest hole near the outskirts of the clearing. I considered using the shovel as a weapon, but we were outnumbered and Biers had a gun. I didn't think we had a choice at this point. If we were digging, at least we'd be alive.

The dig was hard work; I hadn't done any real manual labor since high school, when I volunteered to help build HUD houses for several summers, and the muscles used in digging and building were very different. Grace seemed to be handling it much better than me. Even Jin was doing better, which surprised me. I'd figured him to be a "constantly at his computer" sort of guy. I was wrong, apparently.

"I still don't see how you possibly think you're going to get away with this when it's all said and done," Grace grunted out between shoveling.

"You provided me that out, like I said. You targeted Daniel as the likely killer. I'm sure your condescending, stuck-up friend here—" He gestured at me. "—told his police officer boyfriend of his suspicions, too."

Shit. He was right about that. I didn't say anything, but Biers obviously saw the truth on my face, because he chuckled.

"See, the plan will work. I'll tell everyone that Daniel Rice killed you and took off with the treasure. I was lucky to be left alive. In the meantime, I'll have murdered Daniel and dumped his body in the ocean. By the time anyone finds it—if they ever do—I'll be long gone with the money I made on the black market from selling these goods. It's a damn near perfect plan."

The smart-ass in me wanted to hit him with some quip about how it wasn't a perfect plan, but unfortunately from where I stood, it seemed like it would work.

The digging took at least two hours, but we finally struck something hard and metal.

Biers gave a signal and the seven men crowded down into the hole, ushering Grace, Jin, and me out of it. Biers came to stand next to us, a fire in his eyes. "We've finally found it," he murmured. "After all this time, here it is."

It took another thirty minutes to unearth the top of the thing in its entirety—it was long. Once they did that, they started in on the dirt surrounding it until they'd knocked enough loose to reveal the latch to it.

"Bring me Mr. Rice," Biers instructed one of the men. "He's worked three years to find it; he deserves to see what's inside before he dies."

The man obeyed, fetching Rice and taking him by the elbow and jerking him to his feet. He forced Rice to hop along after him, with his feet bound in a display that could only be called offhandedly cruel. Just as he reached where we stood with Biers, Rice let out a loud shout, throwing himself at Biers and knocking him unsteady.

I didn't hesitate for a moment. "Run!"

Grace and Jin complied, making a break into the nearby tree line before the men in the hole could react.

"I don't suppose you have a plan beyond running?" Grace asked, ducking beneath a branch. "In case you didn't realize, we're on an island."

"We're going to get on the boat and we're going to drive it, pilot it, do whatever it is you do to a boat, and get the hell out of here."

"And leave Rice behind?"

I was having a similar moral quandary, and I'd hoped Grace wouldn't bring it up. "There's nothing we can do for him except get help," I said finally. *If he's still alive by then.* I didn't mention that concern to Grace, though.

We reached the beach and started toward the boat. I could hear the men in pursuit of us crashing through the trees; they would be through any second; there was no time to waste. I cursed the water as we started wading through it; it made my legs feel like heavy, like they were running through jelly, like that feeling of heaviness your legs took on in a dream where you were inevitably fleeing from someone or something. You had to struggle through each step.

Jin reached the boat and paused to help Grace aboard, giving her a boost. He offered to boost me up too, but I waved him away.

"Just get in the boat!"

A look over my shoulder told me we were just about out of time. Biers's men had broken through the trees and were nearly to the water, the boat's driver in the lead. But where was Biers?

Probably stayed behind to keep an eye on his precious tontine, I thought, grabbing the boat and hoisting myself into it.

"The keys are still here," Grace called from the front of the boat. Before I'd even reached her, she had the boat started. "That was way easier than I thought it would be. Now let's see if the driving is as simple."

"You might want to hurry. Those guys are right behind us."

"I know how to drive this thing," Jin said, gently moving Grace aside and taking control. Under his deft hands, the boat began to move, heading away from the people on the beach who'd started toward the second boat in pursuit.

"Nice going, Jin!" Grace threw her arms around him from the side, leaning forward and kissing his cheek.

"How do you know how to drive one of these things, anyway?" I asked, coming up on his other side. I didn't hug him, settling for patting his shoulder.

"My folks taught me when I was a teenager. They're members of the yacht club."

"I didn't realize your parents were rich," Grace said, surprised.

"Well, we're not really that rich."

"We can talk about this later," I said impatiently. "Are we going the right way?"

"I think this is the way we came," Jin said. "We should use the radio to send up a mayday. Maybe the coast guard will hear it."

"That won't be necessary," Edwin Biers said from behind us. We all three nearly jumped, turning to face him, gun in hand. He must have taken the already somewhat worn path to the boats and climbed aboard, hiding below while we got on. He'd known this would be our plan, of course; what else could we have done? "If you'll kindly kill the engine, Mr. Hamada." Jin complied. "Good. Now, take the keys out of the ignition and throw them into the ocean."

Jin hesitated, and Biers cocked the hammer of his gun.

"Do it, Jin," I said shakily. My heart sank when I heard the small splash the keys made in the water before they sank below the surface, taking with them any hope I had of us getting out of this alive.

"What's the plan now, Biers?" Grace asked bitterly. "Are you going to shoot us and drag us back to the island?"

Biers laughed, an altogether unfriendly sound. "Of course not, Ms. Park. You think I don't know that cops will be able to tell you didn't get shot on the island if I do that? That leads to too many questions being asked. I wanted to shoot you on the island and link it to Daniel, which had its inherent risks, I admit. You've provided me with a much more appealing option, though. If the boat sinks and we're all lost at sea, they'll have no problem tallying me among the dead, which limits the chances of them searching for me once I have my money."

"Maka knows about the tontine," I blurted. If there was even the slightest chance that it would make him reconsider his actions, let us go and flee, then I had to take it. Besides, didn't look like we'd be getting money for this contract anyway.

"You think I don't know that? They'll just think that Daniel took it and fled. This really will work much better for me in the long run."

As Biers spoke the second boat from the island pulled up alongside us. "Farewell, people of Paradise Investigations." Biers turned and jumped the short distance between the two boats. The boat started away from us.

"He's just going to leave us stranded?" Jin asked in disbelief. "He realized that we can still radio for—"

Before Jin finished speaking Biers pointed his gun at the boat. Several rounds were fired. I dropped to the deck, covering my head. I couldn't see, but I heard Grace and Jin do the same.

The boat gave a sudden lurch, tilting ever so slightly to the left.

"He shot holes in the boat!" I cried, coming to my feet. I had no idea how many shots they'd fired because I hadn't bothered counting them, but my guess was a lot. We might not have a lot of time.

"He's getting away, and we're going to sink," Grace said, pacing in circles.

"We'll be fine," I assured her. "The island isn't all that far. Maybe we can swim to it."

"And then get shot by Biers? Lovely options!" Grace's voice rose an octave and a half, bordering on hysterical, her eyes bugging out. "The radio! Try the radio!"

"It's broken," Jin called. He'd gone to investigate the radio as soon as it was apparent we were sinking. "No way I can fix it, either."

"Things just keep getting better and better," I growled in impotent rage. I turned to Biers's fleeing boat and threw up my middle finger. "Fuck you, Edwin Biers," I yelled at the top of my voice.

As if to give expression to my rage, four boats came around the island, two on either side, three of them making a run for Biers's boat, the other speeding toward us.

"What now?" Grace moaned, though a moment later her face shifted from despair to hope. The side of one of the boats had come into view. Honolulu Police Department was stamped along the side of it in big golden letters, along with the seal of the police department.

"Is that Maka?" she gasped.

"Yes!" I grinned, waving toward the approaching boat. I had no doubt Maka was aboard. "Just in time, too!"

"How did he find us?" Grace asked, mystified.

I dug into my pocket and pulled out a small oval device. "Maka made me bring this tracking device, said cell phone tracking is unreliable."

"Oh my god, I could kiss him!"

"I would really prefer that you didn't," I said dryly.

"It's just an expression, Gabe."

"Looks like you couldn't help yourselves, just getting into trouble," Maka tutted as the boat he was on came level with ours. "I swear I can't let you guys leave the house, can I?"

"How did you know we were in trouble?" Grace asked, crossing to the police boat first.

"When Gabe's phone went dead, I figured something had happened. I was prepared for it, actually. When we lost the signal, we went into action."

Maka held out a hand, taking mine and pulling me across the gap between boats. I could see the urge to hold me close in his eyes—an urge I shared—but he resisted, and I followed his lead. He was at work, and we would keep things as professional as we could.

I would thank him for riding to the rescue later, when we were alone.

IT WAS A relief to see Honolulu Harbor come into sight. Grace, Jin, and I had given statements to Maka and the other officers, so by the time we reached land, we were all but ready to go home.

I stood on solid ground once more and watched as the police carted Biers and his goons off another boat one by one. I could not deny a great sense of satisfaction watching them being loaded into a line of waiting police cars. Justice had been served.

Daniel Rice was the last to disembark from the police boat. He looked shaken but unharmed. He spotted us and quickly headed our way, weaving through the flurry of policemen coming and going.

"Thank you so much," he said, taking my hand. I was caught off guard by the sincerity of his gratitude. I'd been expecting anger, cursing, maybe even physical violence, but a handshake? Hadn't even crossed my mind.

"You're not upset we suspected you?" Grace asked, voicing my surprise.

"I can't say I blame you for that—I didn't really give you much reason to trust me, the way I acted. The truth is, I didn't trust you all, either, so I guess we're kind of even, yes?"

"That's a very understanding attitude." I agreed.

"One more thing—you did what you promised, so I want to follow through on Edwin's promise. I'm going to pay your contract in full."

I might have gotten whiplash from how quickly my head jerked toward Grace. Her face mirrored mine—shock. I figured we'd be writing this one off as a loss, but if Rice was going to foot the bill...

"Are you sure?" Grace asked. I wanted to slap my hand over her mouth. If Rice decided not to, we'd be in a world of trouble financially.

"I'm sure." Rice turned to watch the police officers unloading the big locker that contained the tontine items. "It was never about taking these items, not for the rest of us. We didn't know Edwin's intentions, or we wouldn't have helped. I know the others would be happy to have it end this way. Well, maybe not exactly this way," he amended, "but close. I'll stop by your office tomorrow morning and settle the contract."

One of the detectives from farther down the docks approached us. "Detective Kekoa, there's a man who'd like to speak to these three." He pointed to Grace, Jin, and me.

"We didn't break any laws, did we?" I asked Maka nervously.

"Just go." Maka took my hand once more and gave it a quick squeeze. "I'll see you at your place when I finish work."

We were met at the end of the dock by two Japanese men in their late fifties. One had gray, thinning hair, the other's hair remained black. They both wore suits and were flanked by a security team. I noticed a black government sedan parked not far away.

The gray-haired man spoke. "These are the people responsible for the return of these artifacts to the Japanese people?"

"Yes, sir," the police officer who led us there answered.

Both men gave us low, formal bows. Still bent in the bow, the gray-haired man addressed us. "On behalf of the Japanese people, we offer you our sincerest thanks. You do not know what it means to have these artifacts returned to our people."

"We're glad we could be of service, sir," I said.

The men straightened, extending their hands, and we all shook. The moment was surreal; I'd never met a representative of a foreign government before. "There is an organization that offers a reward for any artwork or items appropriated from Japanese possession during the war. I will ensure they have your names and that the reward is given to you as expediently as possible."

Goodbyes were made, and the men returned to the dark car, no doubt going to the Japanese embassy to arrange the return of the tontine.

"Doesn't it feel good, having helped those people?" Grace asked, throwing an arm over my shoulder.

"It does," I admitted as we began to make our way toward Grace's Jeep. "I've never thought of you as the purely altruistic type, Grace. You've surprised me today."

"Well, it will feel good to get that reward money, too."

I chuckled. "There's the Grace I know."

Epilogue

SITTING AT MY desk in the late afternoon sunlight, thinking about the whole matter, I was reminded of something that my grandfather told me plenty of times before. "Everything finds its way to where it belongs, eventually. Things happen the way they are meant to."

Thinking about how Biers was behind bars, the contents of the tontine on their way back to Japan where they belonged, and with the generous reward the Japanese government provided us for ensuring their return in the Paradise Investigations bank account, I couldn't help but agree with him.

I wound up in Hawaii, and then I wound up with Maka, and then I wound up being business partners with my best friend. I'd say that all worked out pretty damn well.

The paperwork on the whole tontine debacle was done and filed, and I was ready to put it behind me. Turning in my chair to look out the window at the cloudless blue Hawaiian sky, though, I couldn't help but get the feeling that this place wasn't quite done with me yet.

And I was actually okay with that.

About the Author

J. C. Long is an American expat living in Japan, though he's also lived stints in Seoul, South Korea—no, he's not an army brat; he's an English teacher. He is also quite passionate about Welsh corgis and is convinced that anyone who does not like them is evil incarnate. His dramatic streak comes from his lifelong involvement in theatre. After living in several countries aside from the United States, J. C. is convinced that love is love, no matter where you are, and he is determined to write stories that demonstrate exactly that. J. C. Long's favorite things in the world are pictures of corgis, writing, and Korean food (not in that order...okay, in that order). J. C. spends his time when not writing by thinking about writing, coming up with new characters, attending Big Bang concerts, and wishing he was writing. The best way to get him to write faster is to motivate him with corgi pictures. Yes, that is a veiled hint.

Facebook: www.facebook.com/authorjclong

Twitter: @j_c_long_author

Website: www.jclong.org/

Email: jclongauthor@gmail.com

Also by J.C. Long

Unzipped Shorts
New Year's Even Unzipped
Unzipping 7D

Hong Kong Nights Series
A Matter of Duty
A Matter of Courage

Gabe Maxfield Mysteries
Mai Tais and Murder
Hula Dancers and Hauntings

Recently Released from J.C. Long

Hula Dancers and Hauntings

Gabe Maxfield Mysteries, Book 2.5

Excerpt

"HAVE YOU READ this article in today's paper?" Grace Park asked from where she lounged on the black leather couch that decorated the waiting room at Paradise Investigations.

"You know I avoid the paper at all costs," Gabe Maxfield replied dryly. He paced back and forth in front of the secretary's desk, looking at the clock on the wall once every three seconds or so.

"Apparently, there's been another body found in the suburbs," Grace said, obviously ignoring Gabe's lack of interest. There was nothing new about that, though; it seemed to be Grace's default operating mode. "Some sort of wild animal attack, they're saying. Isn't that weird, Gabe?"

"I guess so," Gabe agreed, though he hadn't even really been paying attention to what she was saying. They had one more client supposedly coming in, but they were running late.

"You're so damn antsy," Grace chided. "Chill out. We've got plenty of time. Your date with Maka isn't for another three hours. We've never had a consultation last that long. You're just working yourself into a state over nothing."

He knew Grace was right, but that just made it worse for some reason. He hated the idea of being late for a date, especially since Maka had been very busy recently and their chances for date nights had decreased exponentially, even though they literally lived next door to each other.

"I don't want to risk the date going south," he said, his feet not stopping their pacing. "The last date we had I kind of screwed up by falling asleep."

Grace quirked an eyebrow lewdly. "I always assumed Maka was great in bed."

"Not like that!" Gabe could feel a blush coming on, but fought through it. "He rented a scary movie, and I fell asleep during it. You know how I am with scary movies."

Grace cringed. "Classic mistake. Didn't you tell him you're basically impossible to scare?"

Gabe shook his head. "No. He's really into Halloween and the scares, so I didn't want to rain on his parade. The plan was to pretend to be scared, but the movie got the best of me. I would like Halloween so much more if I could actually be scared."

"There's plenty to Halloween besides the cheap scares. Like getting drunk!"

"The last time I was drunk with Maka, I tried to get a dead pig's head into his car," Gabe reminded her. "I'm not all that eager to repeat the experience."

Gabe looked at the clock once more and sighed. "I'm giving this mystery client five more minutes and then I'm leaving."

"This is the third time she's forgotten to write down a caller's name," Grace said pointedly, sitting up. She was merely rehashing an old argument they'd had more times than either of them would care to admit. Grace didn't like Mrs. Neidermeyer, and that wasn't going to change. "You need to talk to her. You're the one who hired her, after all."

Gabe said nothing, knowing it would do no good. The secretary argument wasn't going away any time soon, and he'd come to accept that.

"Oh, someone's coming now," Grace said, standing up to get a better look through the blinds on the front window.

"Finally," Gabe muttered, relaxing visibly. He was ready to get this consultation done so he could get home and make the last bad date they'd had up to Maka. The last person he expected to see walk through the doors was Hiapo.

A mountain of a man at nearly a foot taller than Gabe and three times as wide, Hiapo ran an exclusive and very popular lū'au spot there on the island. Instead of the Aloha-print shirt Gabe was used to seeing him in, Hiapo was wearing an orange shirt with black witch hats, bats, and pumpkins in honor of Halloween, which was six days away.

"Howzit, bruddah?" Hiapo grinned at them.

"You're our three thirty?" Grace asked, greeting him with a big, warm hug.

"More like our four o'clock," Gabe corrected, though his words lacked ire.

They decided to take the meeting out front where Hiapo could sit comfortably on the couch. Grace and Gabe dragged chairs over and they began.

"Why exactly are you looking for PI services, Hiapo?" Gabe asked once he was settled.

"I've had three hula girls quit in the last two days, that's why." He had the barest hint of a growl in his words. "One quit about three hours ago—that's why I was late, trying to find their replacements."

From Gabe's experiences with Hiapo's lū'au, his employees were really happy. Hiapo provided a great work environment and was just an all-around nice guy. "Why are they quitting so suddenly? Is there inter-employee strife?"

"Nah, nothing like that, brat. Weird stuff's been happening at the lū'au." Hiapo lowered his voice a little. "Things moving or going missing. The girls say they feel like somebody's been watching them. There's strange noises coming from the woods around the place. The girls are convinced it's haunted."

Grace, who loved all things paranormal or haunted, looked absolutely intrigued. Gabe wasn't so easily impressed, though. "You do realize that PI stands for *private investigator* and not *paranormal investigator*, right? I mean, this isn't exactly our field of expertise, Hiapo."

"I know it ain't ghosts, bruddah," Hiapo said flatly, like Gabe had insulted him with even the implication that he believed the hype. "What I think's happening is one of my competitors is screwing around with me, trying to hurt my business. I want you two to catch them in the act."

Gabe caught Grace's eye and could see she wasn't having the same doubts he was, but he couldn't help it. This simply didn't sound like something they would be very good at.

Hiapo must have seen Gabe's uncertainty on his face. "I didn't want to do this, cuz, but you owe me after the beach."

Gabe shouldn't have been surprised Hiapo brought that up, but he was. However, surprised or not, he couldn't argue the point. He owed Hiapo more than he could ever hope to repay after what he did for him that night on the beach.

"Okay, because I owe you one."

"Great! Tonight we close at—"

"Not tonight," Gabe interrupted. "I have a date tonight. The earliest we can do it is tomorrow night."

Hiapo nodded. "Okay, you got a deal. And you can both consider yourselves invited to tomorrow night's lū'au—on the house."

"We're still charging you," Grace warned.

Gabe snorted. "Do you know how much it costs to go to Hiapo's lū'au? He's overpaying. A *lot*."

Also Available from NineStar Press

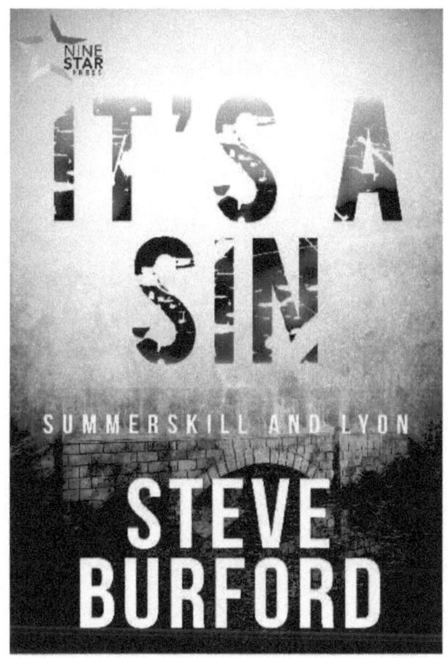

Connect with NineStar Press

www.ninestarpress.com

www.facebook.com/ninestarpress

www.facebook.com/groups/NineStarNiche

www.twitter.com/ninestarpress

www.tumblr.com/blog/ninestarpress